BEYOND REALITIES
VOL II

ANTHOLOGY
OF THE LUNA PRESS PUBLISHING
"WRITERS & ILLUSTRATORS CONTEST"

EDITED BY ROBERT S MALAN

Cover © Jane Stewart 2016
Stories © is with each individual author 2016
Editorial © Robert S Malan 2016

First published by Luna Press Publishing 2016

WWW.LUNAPRESSPUBLISHING.COM

ISBN-13: 978-1-911143-12-3

CONTENTS

FOREWORD

SCIENCE FICTION

BEYOND FICTION   1
By Sarah Dixon
PURE   24
By Sarah Hitchcock
THE WELL-DECEIVED   47
By Joanna Richardson

FANTASY

SPIRIT OF THE FOREST   65
By Pauline E. Dungate
MISTRESS OF FORTUNE   86
By Kim Gravell
THE ONE-ARMED BANDIT   110
By Barbara Stevenson

DARK FANTASY

SUGAR CUBE   125
By Joseph Degand
THE NAUTILUS SHELL   142
By David Steven Malone
THE SESSION   164
By Nina Oram
PET   175
By Valentine Williams

AUTHORS' BIOGRAPHIES   182

FOREWORD

Welcome to the second volume of Beyond Realities.

Beyond Realities, the Writers and Illustrators Contest, was created to introduce Luna Press to authors and artists of SF, Fantasy and Dark Fantasy and, in turn, usher them into the path of a wider audience.

I am thrilled to once more be able to present ten new fascinating stories to you, along with an enchanting cover illustration, and introduce you to their creators.

Senior Editor Robert S Malan and his team worked hard with the authors over the summer preparing this volume, and thoroughly enjoyed the process – just one of the reasons why we love our editorial team!

In January, Luna Press will be two years old. So much has happened in that time that we can scarcely believe it. A huge thank you to you, our readers, for allowing us to do what we love most: writing, publishing and changing perceptions, one word at a time. We'll keep at it!

So take a seat, relax, and let your journey, *beyond reality*, begin.

Thank you,
Francesca T. Barbini

NOTE:
THE ANTHOLOGY IS DIVIDED INTO THE THREE
GENRES OF THE CONTEST:
SCIENCE FICTION, FANTASY & DARK FANTASY.
WITHIN EACH SECTION, THE STORIES ARE
PRESENTED IN ALPHABETICAL ORDER BASED
ON AUTHOR'S SURNAME.

SCIENCE FICTION

BEYOND FICTION

By Sarah Dixon

I come to work in disguise. It's a condition of my employment; when entering or exiting the building, I should dress as though I were an employee of a risk analysis company. I'm not quite sure what to wear that really screams "statistician" so I opt for chain store office wear. I change the moment I'm inside my own office.

Working at PUI is a surreal experience. It's been a couple of weeks now and I'm still waiting for someone to tell me the whole thing has been an elaborate practical joke. I still struggle to believe that the things they tell me I do are even possible.

But, let me start from the beginning …

I'd gotten used to rejection. It's a rite of passage for a writer, friends told me. They tried to raise my spirits by sharing websites that tell you how many times famous authors were rejected before they finally got their publishing contract. J D Salinger, H G Wells, James Joyce; they all had their fair share of criticism and went on to achieve greatness. I knew my friends meant well; they believed in me; I believed in myself, but publishing is a competitive world, and getting into print can be more about luck than skill.

I was a fulltime writer. I kept the wolf from the door through freelance work; using my skills to make dry business documents more engaging, which paid the bills and gave me the flexibility to continue writing the thing that I love: crime novels.

I'm not sure where the fascination with crime started. Maybe it was with the Famous Five and Secret Seven, or the endless repeats of Columbo and Murder She Wrote on afternoon TV when I bunked off school. Whatever it was, I'd always enjoyed reading about crime, fact and fiction, and that naturally led to me wanting to write my own.

I'd had some moderate success: won a short story competition or two, and I self-published my first novel as an eBook, which sold a few hundred at the bargain price of 49p, until someone left me a really punishing review.

I had a blog where I talked about my own writing, and shared what was happening in the world of crime-writing generally. I had the idea that I might raise my profile - fake it 'til I make it; that if I acted like a "proper" writer, success would follow.

Then, one day, I opened my email and found a message with the subject, "Reputable business seeking authors, all genres". I thought at first that it was just another self-publishing house hoping to make a fast buck from me, but the way the message was worded was different from the usual spam; there were no promises of cover design, or marketing, or forecasts of sales figures. There was no mention of a company name at all. The email simply read, "*You have been selected to submit audition pieces for consideration by our company. The audition process involves writing five short pieces in response to set prompts within a time limit. To apply, click this link.*"

I clicked, without too much expectation. I'd heard about websites that ask you to write audition pieces, usually news articles, and keep asking you to resubmit as a way of harnessing the hopes of wannabe authors to generate their text; content farms. This website didn't have the "desperately trying to be hip", overly busy style of those, though.

It had a slick, corporate feel to it; muted colours and stylish lines. The logo contained the initials PUI, possibly an acronym, but there was no definition of it. The contact details were minimal: an email address, a phone number, and a PO Box. They had no social media presence, no blog or Twitter feed, no YouTube channel.

Switching to another window, I plugged "PUI" and "writing" into Google, but only got results of people by the name of PUI, or about writing for Predominantly Undergraduate Institutions. Whatever this website was, it didn't have the perpetually underfunded feel of academia.

There was a link to further information on the audition process, and another to start it. I looked at the FAQ first, but I was more interested in what it didn't say than what it did. There was no further information on the company, or what they did, other than an admission that they were not a publisher and that all writing would remain "in-house", whatever that meant. If it hadn't been for their more in-depth definitions of genres, I'd have thought I was looking at a regular source of corporate freelance work; but they were very clear: they wanted fiction.

There would be five pieces to write for the audition, one each in the genres of Science Fiction, Historical, Mystery/Crime, Romance and Politics/Conspiracy. The website assured me that writers wouldn't be expected to excel in all areas, but that we shouldn't allow lack of experience in any particular genre to put us off submitting; they wanted to see how we responded to themes we were unfamiliar with.

A ghost-writing company, I decided. They were looking for competent writers who would create fiction for other people to put their names to. Bitterness swirled in my stomach at the thought of it: some vacant reality TV star taking credit for my creativity. But the promise of excellent rates of pay, and regular, flexible hours, had me swallowing my pride.

The audition process was simple: for each genre, you would click through, see a prompt, and then have up to two hours to create a short piece of fiction in response. It might have made some writers quail, but it was perfect for me. I have no shortage of ideas. I've never had writer's block. The slightest little whiff of inspiration can set me off; I'm like a radio, picking up stories from all over the world. It doesn't feel like I make these things up; more like tuning in to a situation, as though my mind somehow transports to different places and I'm watching something that is actually happening. My fingers race to try and record it all before it fades out. The story often feels more real than actual reality. It's hard to explain; have you ever had one of those dreams that you wake from and can't quite shake off, even though you know, rationally, that it didn't happen? It's like that. Absorbing and compelling.

I wrote their articles over the course of a week, one a day. Some came easier than others; the crime story flowed almost instantly, but historical? I couldn't connect with an idea at all. The portrait that I was given as the prompt didn't really inspire me. I knew it was well written, in as much as it was grammatically correct, and I'd used fresh metaphors; I'm a good writer, but the idea was lacklustre.

Three days later, they sent me another email: my work had potential and they wanted to meet me for a face to face interview. First, though, I had to attend a free health check at a medical facility nearby. This made me feel a little wary. It's not that medicals are unknown as part of the recruitment process; it's just that they tend to come *after* the interview, once an offer has been made. I wondered why they were doing it this early; maybe the job involved a lot of foreign travel, or there had been problems in the past with drug or alcohol addiction? Creative types are often flawed.

I had nothing to hide, so I made the appointment as soon as possible and cleared my diary for the day so I could go along. The medical facility was private and in one of the new office developments that had sprung up on the edge of town;

it was so new, in fact, that it hadn't put its proper signage up yet. A laminated sheet of A3 was attached to the sign by the entrance, and a simple piece of A4 was stuck in the window; both said, "PUI Medical".

There was no receptionist, just a doorbell on the desk that said to press for attention. I pressed, hearing a dull echo of a bell from behind a door.

A man in a white coat startled me by pushing the door open just a few seconds later. He greeted me warmly and led me to his office, introducing himself as Doctor Watson. I laughed, out of politeness, when he assured me he had nothing to do with Mr Holmes. It felt like one of those rehearsed lines designed to set people at ease. On the other side was a large, open plan office space; only, where I would have expected desks and chairs, there was an array of medical equipment.

He started with familiar tests, measuring my height and weight, taking my blood pressure; but after that, things took a bit of a strange turn. Doctor Watson took a net of what looked like electrodes - sticky rubber pads on the end of wires - and put them at certain points over my head.

'An EEG?' I asked.

'Not exactly. Similar.'

'Oh …' I wanted to know more, but I sensed he was being evasive. Perhaps he thought I wouldn't understand anything too technical. 'What does this tell PUI, then?'

Doctor Watson attached the last electrode, stepped back, and gave me a reassuring smile. 'Just how remarkable your brain is.'

I frowned, because it wasn't really an answer, and I wasn't sure how to continue the conversation without being rude. But he had already turned away, and called over his shoulder, 'Do you prefer pen and paper, or a computer, to write with?'

'Computer, please.'

He nodded and diverted his path towards a trolley with

a computer set on it. As he pushed it back towards me, he explained, 'You need to write something; don't worry, it isn't going to be sent to PUI as a sample; it's just for use here in the examination. Please write a crime story; your prompt is …' He patted his pockets as though he had forgotten where he had put something, then produced a photograph. '… this.'

I reached out to take it, and held it at arm's length to get an overview. It was a passport type photograph of a young woman, maybe 25 years old. Pretty, not wearing any make up, but there was something hesitant in her eyes; haunted, even.

I connected with her immediately; it happens like that sometimes with a story. As I looked at the photograph, I gained a sense of knowing her; I heard her voice speaking directly to me. I nodded absently, scooting closer to the keyboard and letting my fingers fly as I recorded the story that she was telling me.

There were tears on my cheeks when I was done. I hadn't even noticed that I'd shed them. Blinking back to reality, the world didn't feel quite right, as if I was waking from a dream, or reality had subtly changed whilst I'd been tuned out. Glancing around, I saw that Doctor Watson was perched on a chair nearby, watching the display and sipping a glass of water.

'You're all done.'

It wasn't a question; it was a statement. I nodded, clearing my throat. The display told me I'd written almost 3,000 words. That must have taken two hours at least. The stiffness in my shoulders reinforced the passage of time.

'I'm sorry; did I take too long?'

'Oh no, no. That was really useful. I collected some valuable data.'

'Can I ask what for?'

'I'm sworn to secrecy,' Watson explained. 'I could tell you but I'd have to kill you and all that.' He smiled, but seemed to realise his humour had fallen flat. 'I mean, the application of the data is commercially sensitive. You'll learn more once you've had your face to face interview.'

Glancing back to the photograph of the girl, I was torn between feeling guilty that my imagination had conjured up such a grisly fate for her, and a sense that I'd given her a voice somehow.

The medical was over soon after that. Doctor Watson couldn't, or wouldn't, give me any more information, other than to say that PUI would be in touch soon.

An email arrived the next day, inviting me to an interview at their central London offices, providing I was willing to sign a non-disclosure agreement. I was still plagued with doubts that this was some obscure, vanity publishing scam. The truth is that aspiring authors don't get feted by anyone in the industry; that only happens once you've proven yourself a money-maker, over and over again.

The outside of the PUI building was as enigmatic as everything else about them: smoky grey glass that hid what went on inside from view, whilst allowing them to look out. The brass plaque simply said "PUI"; still no expansion on what the acronym might stand for. I took a deep breath before I stepped inside, a polite five minutes before the appointment time. A chic receptionist, guessing who I was, greeted me, then asked me to sit in the comfortable waiting area until Sasha, the person I was meeting, was ready. While I was waiting, could I read and sign the non-disclosure agreement?

Even in here, there were no answers. No digital photo frames cycling through projects that PUI had been involved in; no framed certificates of their achievements. The low coffee table had no literature on it; only a carafe of water, a few glasses and a small bowl of mints. I helped myself, sipping slowly as I read through a fairly standard NDA, and added my scrawl to the bottom.

'Jennifer?'

I started as my name was spoken, spilling a little cold water on my skirt and stifling a curse at my clumsiness. I could feel colour rising in my cheeks as I rose, reached for a napkin to dry my hands, and faced Sasha for the first time. My embarrassment only grew as I took in the sheer perfection of her: she was a blonde Audrey Hepburn, timelessly beautiful and effortlessly stylish.

'Oh. Yes. Hello,' Between her poise and my nerves, I'd been robbed of my eloquence. I gave myself a beat to recover. 'I'm Jennifer. You must be Sasha?'

'I am,' she confirmed, her good breeding made obvious in the ease with which she ignored my clumsiness and discomfort.

'Would you like to come with me?' she asked, as she picked up the clipboard and completed the form.

I followed Sasha through a door to the side of the reception desk, admiring her manicure as she swiped her ID card to get us access. We stepped into a corridor with rooms to either side; there was the low murmur of conversation and the aroma of good coffee. Whatever PUI did, there was no shortage of money to it; at least based on appearances.

Sasha guided me into the first room on the right, a conference room with a long, highly polished black table, set out with chairs on all sides. Conference phones were placed at intervals, and there was a large video screen attached to one wall.

'Can I get you a coffee?' Sasha asked.

'Yes please,' I said, as I took the seat she gestured to, hoping that I did so with a fraction of her natural grace.

'We're going to start by watching a short video that gives you an overview of PUI. After that, you'll no doubt have some questions.'

My forehead furrowed at the certainty in her tone, but I

nodded and settled back to watch the screen. Seconds later, the PUI logo was revealed and a female narrator began to speak.

'Welcome to PUI, where art and science combine.' I glanced towards Sasha, but she was busy making coffee with the indifference of one who had heard this pitch a thousand times. 'PUI was founded more than a decade ago by twin brothers, Samuel and Leonard Conway. These unique individuals were both quickly identified as gifted by their school system, but their gifts were in radically different areas. While Samuel had a gift for understanding the arts, Leonard had a natural affinity for quantum physics.'

Left and right brain, I thought, leaning forward a little as the story began to engage me; as the narrator spoke, images were displayed on the screen, the visual prompt bringing the people to life in my mind; I felt the tug of the narrative.

'During their post-graduate studies, a late night debate over the relative merits of their fields led to a breakthrough in our understanding of the world around us.'

Sasha slid a coffee in front of me, but I barely noticed; I was too busy trying to work out where the story was going.

'Samuel's work dealt mainly in analysis of recurring motifs in folk stories from around the world; Leonard was working on a thesis based on Many Worlds Theory. Sharing their research gave them the unique perspective that underpins PUI today and led to the formation of a company that now works with governments, companies and individuals worldwide to solve problems.'

I absently reached for my coffee. I wanted them to cut to the chase: what did they do? Why might they want me to work for them?

'The Conway Brothers collaborated on research which led to a remarkable discovery: creative inspiration was not as random as had previously been thought. Certain writers actually possessed the ability to transcend the natural borders between moments in time, or parallel universes. They weren't making things up, but were simply accessing a different part of their consciousness.'

I gave out a coffee-tinged splutter of disbelief, and turned to find Sasha watching me with amusement. I was half tempted to leave but, whatever their business was, it seemed lucrative, and getting a regular income with enough spare time to write a novel was 'the dream'.

'By developing technology that monitors the brainwaves of writers, we are able to determine, within a great degree of statistical probability, whether the 'story' they create is simply that, or contains information gleaned from the past, the future, or alternate realities.'

'PUI is now part of the decision-making process in some of the most critical choices facing our world; from the personal micro-level - locating missing persons, or solving crimes - to the macro; what is the likely outcome of a particular technological advancement or commercial decision.'

It hit me, all of a sudden, that this must be a joke, an elaborate set up. I glanced around for cameras, but couldn't see anything obvious. I looked to Sasha again, holding what I hoped was just the right amount of challenge in my eyes. She reached for a remote control and hit pause.

'You tested positively for the ability to write about the present.'

'Tested?'

'A combination of brainwave analysis from your medical, and your response to the prompts we gave you.'

'That … that was just fiction!'

Sasha simply smiled patiently, as though she was waiting for me to catch up.

'Are you trying to say I have some sort of … psychic powers?'

'I know it's a lot to take in, but most writers who come on

board with us describe how, in a way, they had always known; they had always experienced a sense of … relocation, when they wrote, as though their minds travelled without them.'

I slumped with the realisation that she was putting into words a sensation I was very familiar with: the *tuning in*.

'You understand the non-disclosure agreement now? This is proprietary technology: we don't want even the ideas falling into the wrong hands.'

'How do you know someone isn't writing about them right now?' I asked, flippantly.

'We closely monitor fiction,' Sasha replied as though I had asked the most normal question in the world.

I ruffled my hair, destroying the carefully groomed style I had hoped would impress the good people at PUI. I understood now that they were far, far more interested in my mind.

'How does it work?'

'Much as it did with your audition: we give you a prompt and you respond to it according to how it inspires you. Let's say we were asking you to locate a missing shipment; you would have as much information about it as possible, to set the scene; what it looked like, what was in it, where it was last seen, who might want it. Then we'd ask you to tell the story. A number of other writers - how many will depend on the budget of the client - will also respond. Common themes are identified, coming up with a "most likely scenario", which then guides the client.'

My jaw worked as I shook my head, trying to fundamentally deny what she was saying.

'That … I mean, this can't be science. Yes, there are recurring motifs in stories. Cultural bias will affect the response to prompts. If you tell me about a drunk girl leaving a club in the early hours, there are bound to be common themes in what anyone, not just writers, would tell you about what happened.'

'Our equipment allows for that.'

It wasn't so much what Sasha said that was so compelling, but the certainty that underpinned every word; the fact that she had that response so readily to hand, that she must have had this same conversation countless times with other people.

'This is real?' I asked, after a moment.

'It is,' she agreed, watching my expression closely. I'm sure she could see the disbelief that was still at the forefront of my mind.

'How?'

Sasha let out a wry chuckle. 'I can't say that I understand it myself; the physics is highly complicated. They talk about string theory and frequencies, but it's all beyond me. All I know is that I've seen it work.'

I took a moment to collect my thoughts; there was a part of me that was still looking for the camera, expecting a TV presenter to pop out from behind a door, along with my brother or an old friend, all convulsed with laughter that I fell for it. There was another part of me that fundamentally accepted what she said as being true, because it so accurately reflected my own experience. There was also a part of me that had one, big, question: 'If this were true, wouldn't we have heard about it by now? Nobel prizes, scientific papers, corporate advertising. Why are you keeping it so secret?'

'Ultimately because the Conways are very ethical people,' Sasha said.

Before I was able to censor them, my brows shot upwards in obvious disbelief. There aren't many heads of corporations as slick as PUI seemed to be, who could claim to be ethical.

'I know, it's unusual, but they are.' Sasha slid into a seat opposite me, settling herself comfortably as she explained, 'They're remarkable people. They realised as soon as they made their discovery that it had tremendous potential for abuse, and they wanted to do what they could to ensure that didn't happen. Can you imagine if someone unprincipled wanted to ensure they won an election, for example? Our writers could, potentially, work out how to make that happen.'

'Really?'

'Really. Ask any conspiracy author to write a scenario in which someone highly improbable found their way into elected office. They would do it. It would be an intricate plot, with pressure applied in just the right places. Perhaps murder, or false-flag terrorist acts, but an unprincipled person wouldn't care what it took to influence the people: they'd only care about the end result. If PUI were only motivated by money …' Sasha left me to finish that thought myself.

I blinked a few times, trying to clear the cognitive dissonance that I was actually having this conversation. Feeling the pull between what I thought was possible and what I knew of the power of stories.

'So how do they ensure that their secret is kept?'

'By not telling it. At least not in full,' Sasha explained. 'Anyone who knows even as much as you do, has to sign a non-disclosure agreement; but more than that, we've already had our people assess the risk. If the analysis of your "story" had shown significant risk to PUI, you would not have been given this interview.'

'I was a prompt for one of your writers?'

'You were.' Sasha smiled, and continued to watch my reactions with a sense of amusement, like Alice watching someone else go down the rabbit hole.

'You do the same for clients, I suppose?'

Sasha shrugged. 'On occasion, but usually we use one of our explanation scenarios; these are narratives that have been constructed to give an adequate explanation without causing anyone to investigate our methods too closely. Often, for example, we will talk about mathematics experts, game theory, or high level statistical modelling.'

'You lie?'

'We do. The sorts of truths that we discover are sharp instruments, Jennifer. Lethal in the wrong hands.'

My eyes wandered over Sasha's face, looking for something to anchor me in a world that had suddenly dropped out of focus.

'Why do you tell your writers what they're doing? Why not keep them in the dark too, let them think they're writing fiction?'

'We tried that, in the beginning.' I thought I saw a trace of approval in her expression for the question. 'The bottom line was; results weren't so good. We find that writers have better results if they recognise the sensation of truly connecting; if they trust that and wait for it. It seems to stop them getting caught up in something that is really just an idea - true fiction.'

The lipstick I had generously applied helped my lips slide as I pressed them together. I allowed myself a few more seconds to process what had been said, feeling my thoughts slowly settle around this new reality.

'What is it like to be a PUI writer?' I asked.

'As you can imagine, it's not really a 9-5 job. Particularly for your speciality, where there can often be deadlines. Those who look back don't usually have to rush. It's rarely important to immediately know the truth of something that happened hundreds of years ago. Likewise, for the future; decisions can often be postponed until we have a reasonable degree of certainty. For mysteries, crimes, robberies, that kind of thing, the deadlines can be quite immediate.'

'That's when you pull an all-nighter?' I suggested.

Sasha nodded. 'We generally ask writers to stay for as long as the inspiration is flowing. You'll come to realise when you can help, and when you can't. We encourage writers to go home and rest, even if there is a deadline, when there isn't a good flow of ideas. Otherwise, it just wastes everyone's time.'

'Where do writers work? From home?'

'No, from their own office here at PUI. It'll have whatever you need to promote your creativity: a view, a balcony, music, a couch, a bed, a desk … one writer has a sensory deprivation tank.'

'Why from here? I mean, where I write varies, depending on what I'm writing or whether I'm editing. When writing, I like to be home alone, in silence, but when I'm editing, I like a coffee shop or to be outside.'

'We have a coffee shop!' Sasha said, eyes sparkling at my reaction. 'It's open to the public, on the other side of this building so it doesn't seem to be connected, but you can go and sit there and soak up the atmosphere, if it helps. One writer has a projector, and he chooses a webcam to display on his office wall; it makes him feel like he's travelling all over the world while he stays in one place.'

'And how does payment work?'

'You'd be paid a retainer, to be on call in case we need you for something, then there are bonuses associated with each project. We have enough clients that you can make this a full time job, if it suits you, or you can pick and choose from available jobs. But …' She broke off, pausing for a moment, as if she was debating what she might say next. '… if you're as good as your initial testing predicted, you'll be very much in demand.'

I felt the stretch in my forehead as my surprise at her comment registered on my face.

'Oh. I … I'm not sure what to say to that.'

Sasha smiled. 'You know, we call this an interview, and that usually means that the interviewee, you, comes and persuades the employer, us, that you're the right person for the job. It's not quite like that today. We already know that you're the right person for us. My job was really to convince you that PUI is real, and that you belong here. Is there anything else that I can say, any more questions, or would you like some time?'

For the first time I noticed traces of anxiety in her expression. She didn't seem at all sure what my decision was going to be.

'Who decides if what they're doing is the right thing?' I asked. 'Who decides what's ethical?'

Sasha nodded, a tacit approval of the question. 'Ultimately, it's the decision of the board, with the Conways having the most influence, of course.'

I thought about it, leaned back in the chair, reached for the coffee cup and took a sip, buying myself some more time as I considered. I wasn't sure about the Conways setting themselves up as gatekeepers of this technology, but didn't all companies operate at the whim of the board? I'd worked for companies that had good ethics and bad ethics in the past; I wondered if I was overanalysing, because Sasha had made a point about the Conway's being "good".

Above all, I felt like I was in a dream; as though, if I were to walk out of there, I would wake up and realise that it couldn't be true. That if I didn't say yes, right then, I would have lost the opportunity.

'I'm interested. Very interested,' I said suddenly, committing myself to a course of action.

'Fantastic!' Sasha seemed genuinely relieved and pleased. 'Let's get the paperwork taken care of then …'

One month later, I push open the doors of PUI, call a familiar hello to the receptionist and use my own swipe card to gain access to the inner sanctum. I love the feeling of having access to something so secret that even the people who have paid for the service have no idea what their money bought.

The swipe card gives me, and only me, access to my office on the second floor; a rectangular room with glass all along the opposite wall, that has a view of the street outside. I find watching people going about their business quite soothing. If I feel the need to cut myself off, I just shut the blinds. The wooden floor is warm to the touch of bare feet; I like to write without shoes. I chose a chaise lounge, a large armchair and a desk. I use a laptop so I can work anywhere.

Through a door to the right is a bathroom complete with whirlpool spa bath, and rain-shower. To be honest, asking for those had really been a test of PUI's promise to create the perfect writing environment for me; they delivered. They've also put in a water dispenser and a bean-to-cup machine. There are cupboards full of my favourite snacks. In all honesty, it's writer's heaven.

If the solitude isn't working for me, I can leave my office and try one of the communal areas; the library for silent but companionable working, the snug for a little noise, or of course the coffee shop if I need the buzz and stimulation of the outside world.

I enjoy working for PUI a lot, but I haven't really got to the point of believing in the technology. I'm prepared to overlook my doubts for the pay-check, the benefits, and of course the chance to write fulltime. They don't mind if I spend the day on my novel, or if I'm writing for them. Writers are treated like rare birds, cosseted, indulged. "The talent" is a term I've overheard from support staff, when they refer to us.

The work is interesting; the first mystery that I worked on was locating a laptop that had been left on an underground train. It had contained sensitive information; industrial espionage had been suspected, but the story that I told was one of random chance. A good kid in a bad spot saw an opportunity, never thought the data on the computer could be more valuable than the unit itself, and grabbed it. I've been warned that we won't always know how useful our stories have been to clients, but in this case they sent a generous bonus cheque and a bottle of excellent wine to show their gratitude. It felt really good, to be appreciated, but I still struggled with a vague worry that it was all fraudulent; that the positive results were just coincidence.

I make myself a coffee and change out of my business clothes, and into comfortable leggings and a top: writing clothes. Logging into the network brings up a list of current projects looking for writers, but I barely have time to start looking before I'm surprised by a knock on the door.

So far no one had ever interrupted me when I was in my office; I sit for a moment, wishing I had x-ray vision so I could know if someone was there or it if it had been an accidental knock. The answer comes moments later with another knock and I hurry to see who is there. Standing outside is someone I vaguely recognise. I think he's from Sales; a tall, well set man with cafe crème skin and a goatee.

'Jennifer?' he checks.

'Yes?'

'Hi. I'm Dan. Can I have a word with you about a priority project that's just come in?'

I shrug and gesture for him to come in, retaking my seat at the desk before realising that I don't have a spare seat to offer him. He bypasses my concerns by perching on the corner of the desk, just perfectly at the outside limit of my personal space. There's a pleasant aroma of aftershave coming from him; something musky but citrus light.

'We have a missing persons' case that we'd like you to work on, but it's high pressure. Because you're still relatively inexperienced, I wanted to talk to you about it rather than just add it to your schedule on the system.'

'OK.' I watch him as I reach for my coffee and take a sip, hoping the caffeine will help me work my way through the situation.

'There's a missing child, a little girl, in the USA. At the moment we're not sure if she's just got lost, or been abducted by her biological father or … something far worse.'

My brow furrows in concern. My immediate desire is to help, but Dan holds up a hand to stall me.

'Your instinct is to help, but my job is to look after you.' My cynical side decides PUI just want to keep me working as efficiently as possible. 'Missing child cases are about as emotional as this work gets,' he explains, 'and in this case we don't know that it isn't something more … disturbing. How would you feel about writing … darker material, knowing what you know?'

I suck in a deep breath, letting it out slowly as I consider the question. My instinct is still to say that it's fine, I can handle it, but I want to give myself a moment to really think it through. This is a real little girl; I would know that as I write out the details of her story. What if she'd been abducted by a paedophile, or a psychopath? What if the story that came out of me had a terribly tragic end? How would it feel to know that the parents of this poor child would be told that was most likely what had happened, and all on the basis of my imagination?

But then another thought joins it: what if I don't write anything? What if this little girl is just lost and I can help them find her easily before anything worse than a big scare happens? Could I live with myself if I didn't at least try? What if I really put my faith in what PUI claim they can do?

I look up, noticing that Dan is watching my expression carefully. 'Like I said, we wouldn't normally ask someone so new to this to help, but your results so far have been really impressive and the parents have asked for us to use every resource available. Are you? Available?'

I put my cup down, take a deep breath and let it out slowly, trying to let my intuition guide me. 'Yes, I am.'

Dan's expression forms immediately into a smile. 'Great. I'll have you added to the project. Give us a few minutes and you'll have everything we know so far. Because this is a live case, it's going to work a bit differently. You'll have as much information as possible, to try and eliminate dead ends in the narrative. What you write will be analysed live by the lab. There isn't time for drafting and re-drafting.'

I nod my understanding but, to be honest, that's more because I feel the pressure of the situation and I want some time alone to process it. I potter about my office, getting everything I need in place for a long stretch at my desk. When I return from the bathroom I see an alert on my desktop: I've been assigned the case.

My stomach fills with miniature acrobats as I click to open the file and find myself confronted with an image of a little girl. She's a stereotypical all-American child: blonde hair, blue eyes, pretty with a side order of sassy. She stares into the camera openly, no sign of fear or anxiety. I try to keep my mind open as I look through the other files: a map of the area, along with the statement her parents gave to the police. There's a video too, given at a press conference, but I don't click that; I know it would upset me and I've never written well when I'm emotional. Anyway, it isn't her parents that I want to connect with; it's that sweet girl.

Rotating my shoulders, I take one last, long look at her face and then close my eyes. Leaning back in my seat, I steady my breathing and try to feel the connection that PUI talked about; that moment when it becomes something far more real than a story made up in my head. The moment when it seems to write itself, as though I'm explaining something that has happened, or is happening, elsewhere. My lips curl upwards into a smile as I feel it; I know where she is, and she's all right. She's all right.

I type quickly, not bothering to backspace for typos. I see immediately what has happened, how she had been walking in the fields at the back of her parents' house and seen a lost dog. She'd run after it, because she wanted to help it find its owner but, before she realised it, she was somewhere she'd never been before. All she'd been able to see for miles and miles were tall corn fields and woodland; the dog had disappeared and she'd turned in slow, hopeless circles wondering which way her tired legs should walk to get home.

I try not to waste time on where she's been, to lose myself in the concern that she's had to find a sheltered spot to sleep for the night when it got dark. She's hungry and thirsty; her clothes aren't made for this kind of journey; her dress is getting marked and she's worried her mother will tell her off. I yearn for this communication to be two-way, to let her know somehow that her mother won't care about the dress; that we're coming to get her.

There are landmarks I notice which she wouldn't understand. I'm soon describing a small pond with a fence around it. It belongs to someone. There's a name on the sign that she's too young to read herself, but I can. I put the name in capitals, hoping that will catch the eye of whoever is reading my live feed. I describe electrical pylons marching a line towards a distant farm. I hope as hard as I can that these details will lead the police, or her parents, to find her because I feel her tiredness as though it's my own. She's so young to be going through something like this alone.

I feel her hope surge as she hears the sound of a car engine, and see through her eyes as she turns, trying to locate the direction it came from. Relief rushes through me, filling me with energy as I anticipate a happy ending. I write how she runs headlong over the fields and spills out by the side of a dirt track, causing an old, battered looking van to stop and a man to get out.

Then my heart begins to thud out a warning; I have never felt so hopeless as I watch in a sort of slow motion: the man walks up to the girl and hunkers down to talk to her. There is something so terribly, terribly wrong about the way he is looking at her, his greedy eyes roaming as though she's a meal, or a prize cow. The way he glances around, checking if anyone else is nearby turns my spine to ice. When he invites her into his truck, I groan, biting back frustration as she complies because she is sweet and kind and trusting.

My fingers are flying across the keys but still I can't get the words out fast enough, focussing on any detail of the man, his truck, the road. Finally, he arrives at a house, a shack really, and takes the little girl by the hand, leading her indoors.

I can't bear to follow. I complete my description of the outside, then push myself away from the keyboard like I've been burned. My cheeks are wet with tears; my body aches like a marathon runner limping over the finish line. Looking at the clock I realise that I've been writing without pause for five hours.

I message Dan with, "I need a break" and use the bathroom. Whatever connection I had with the girl had been severed the moment she'd gone inside that house; self-preservation, I think. I hate myself for not having the courage to go where she had to. I shower, trying to scrub off the guilt, then order pizza to be delivered to the reception desk; I need something warm and self-indulgent to chase away the anxiety.

I curl into the chaise lounge, pulling a blanket over me but knowing that the chill I feel isn't physical. I don't know whether I want to believe in PUI and accept that what I've just written is reality, that I might have helped, or hope that it was all fiction. But, if it is fiction, have I just put that poor girl's family through hell with my imagination?

I must have dozed off, because the clock has moved on twenty minutes when I'm roused by another knock on the door. *Pizza*, I think, as I drag myself over to open it. It's Dan, with the familiar square cardboard box, and a reassuring smile.

'She's safe,' he says, stepping into my office and freeing

his hands to wrap me in a warm hug as I start to sob out a physical release of tension. It's the perfect embrace; his strength encases my frailty. His warmth seeps into my core.

'Remind me to bring tissues if I ever have to bring you bad news,' he jokes, as I begin to regain control.

'She's fine?' I check, wiping my cheeks with the back of my hand.

'She's fine. The police got to her about twenty minutes after you'd finished writing. She'd wandered into a neighbouring farm, as you sensed. The cops aren't happy with the guy who found her; he didn't call them.'

'He's not a nice guy,' I say. 'Not at all.' The memories of connecting with his character make me shudder, and Dan slips his arms around me again, warm and reassuring.

'She's safe,' he says again, and I nod. I'm quite happy to let him guide me back to the chaise, and bring me pizza and a drink. He's the perfect companion for this moment, and I wonder if that's his training, or just who he is, as a person. I don't really care either way; I'm just glad he's here.

Once I've recovered a bit, I look up and meet Dan's eyes. 'We do good work here, don't we?'

He nods, his smile warming his expression. 'I think so, yes. It's not always as clear cut as what you've done today but … to be able to do this … you did an amazing thing.'

'I think I'm going to need a few days off.'

Dan chuckles. 'That's fine. Take whatever time you need. If you need anything, well … give me a call. We have therapists on staff to help you, if you want to talk things through, or you and I could just grab a coffee.'

I'm surprised by the little jolt of happiness that runs through me at that invitation. For just a moment I feel the narrative tug at me; what if I take him up on that offer? What if coffee becomes a drink, becomes …

No. What we do at PUI is amazing, but some stories are best left to unfold in their own time.

PURE

BY SARAH HITCHCOCK

'Do you want it or not?'

The agent taps the pass key irritably on her hand. I look at the room: a ten-foot cube of indeterminate metal; no windows – this is deep in the centre of a habitation block. There's a door, through which we're peering, and a bare vent opposite; its grill gone, along with any other fittings that had once been part of the room. There's a drain in the centre of the floor and wires hang from the ceiling. Apertures of various sizes dot the walls. It smells of rusting iron; the smell is like blood.

'I need an answer,' the agent says. 'There are hundreds waiting for a space in the city; hundreds who'd pay more than I'm being told to charge you.'

She regards me with open hostility. Her pupils contract to thin lines and her skin pulses with angry whorls of colour. She's Genem – genetically modified; a hybridised human – as most are now. Pures like me are rare and becoming rarer. My family are pure as far back as we can trace: one of the old clans. Once respected; once part of the elite. My Uncle still holds a council seat in the main hub. It was him who pulled some strings to get me the option on this room. He's the last of us in a position of power. Although, the truth is, his is just a sham office; a pseudo-job. But there are still a few benefits, the occasional obligation owed him. I'm his favourite niece. I think he regards me almost as a pet. I like to think he respects my life choices but, in truth, I think I just amuse him. You see, I am rare even amongst the Pures:

I have resisted enhancements.

Improvement is the norm: implants and replacement parts commonplace; the only limits being the ones imposed by your imagination or your purse. The options range from cosmetic through to altering human capabilities: stronger, faster limbs; more efficient organs; vision in the full spectrum, from infrared to ultraviolet; the ability to see long distances or microscopically; ultra sensitive hearing; computer-assisted thought; microchips to enhance the senses, heighten pleasure receptors, suppression of pain and fear; an unending list of infinite possibilities. What it is to be human is no longer clear; we no longer have a shared identity or common experience. How do you impose a set of rules or laws on such a diverse set of beings? What morals can such variety agree on? Humanity is teetering on chaos and anarchy. And humans like me are regarded with suspicion and, more and more frequently, with the kind of hostility the agent is so openly displaying. I am a freak: subversive, dangerous and, perversely, thought of as unnatural.

'I'll take it,' I say.

The agent slots the pass key into a reader, and I press my thumb to its screen.

'5,000 credits per week. Any default and you will be removed immediately. Full contract and terms will be sent to your com-link in the next hour. You must authorise agreement and supply references by the end of the day. Failure to comply will result in immediate removal and non-refundable debit of one month's rental payment.'

She hands me the key and, with a look of disgust, stalks away down the dimly lit corridor. I watch her cleaning her hands on a cleni-wipe as if to erase the contamination of contact. She tosses the wipe to the floor. The whiteness of it among the filth and litter somehow looks like an accusation; an indictment of my difference.

I step into the box I've just signed off on and dump my

small bag. It's all I was able to bring from the outer province
– a few personal items, a change of clothes and my com-
link. I drag out my old communicator and speak to establish
a connection. The cracked screen fizzes with static but stays
dark, then a voice – bright and heart-achingly familiar – fills
the rusty cube with memories of sunshine, laughing, open
sky.

'Laina, when did you get here? Where the hell are you?
Looks like the inside of a bin. And why can't I feel you? You're
not still using a com are you? God, you're such a dinosaur!'

'Hi, Bel, good to hear you. That's *all* I'm getting though,
no vis. If your plant is so great, how come it's only audio?'

'Shit, sorry, need to make an adjustment; am set up for
plant-to-plant. Hang on …'

The link is broken for a few seconds; just the hiss from
the snow-speckled screen. Broken fragments of sound:
footsteps, or maybe it's a heartbeat; a man's voice, too
muffled to hear words; Bel's voice: 'Yes, it's her …' More
static. A door slams. The sound changes, becomes sharper.

'Is that better?'

I get a vis of a corridor much like the one outside my
room, but cleaner and better lit. I'm seeing what Bel sees.
Long black boots plated with chrome flash in and out of
view as she strides along.

'Let me see you,' she says.

I hold my com up so she can see my face.

'Damn, you're the same! Exactly the same! You haven't
had a thing done, have you?'

'You know how I feel about enhancements.' I start to feel
defensive, but Bel's laugh dispels my misgiving.

'You're such a fossil!'

I laugh with her, but there's something in her tone that
unsettles me: relief? Regret?

'Not fair,' I say. 'I can't see *you*.'

She rounds a corner; ahead of her are polished lift doors

and her grinning reflection pacing toward me. Growing up, she was always a head taller than me, but thin, almost gawky, and athletic. She's filled out, or been filled out, and is voluptuous. Her jerky, feral movements softened; now sinuous and feline. She strikes a pose, hand on hip, and regards herself with a slow smile. Her eyes linger over parts of herself that make me blush.

'Jesu, you're such a narcissist,' I say.

She laughs and draws closer, her reflected face filling the screen.

'WHAT THE HELL IS THAT?'

Something dark, like the coiling tale of a reptile, curls over the contours of her cheek, and its tip slips between her lips.

'It's my tail, darling. What do you think?'

Bel steps back and half-turns; a thick tail whips and swings from beneath her short skirt. She catches hold of the tapered tip and it coils around her hand. It looks leathery but, as she caresses it, goosebumps appear on its black surface, and she shudders.

'It's my latest plant: the deluxe model, packed with sensors tied into my pleasure centres. I won't embarrass you with what it cost ...'

Bel's smile freezes for an instant, and she looks haunted. Then she gives me a wicked leer. 'Hell, darling, if you had a com-plant, we could synch and you'd be able to *feel* this.' She releases the implant and it curls away, disappearing back up her skirt. Her pupils dilate. 'And then you wouldn't have to guess where I keep it!'

'God, you disgusting whore!' I say.

'Don't remember you complaining in the past?'

We both laugh. It feels good to be talking like this with her again. I realise how much I've missed it; missed her. Her reflection leans toward me as she presses the lift call. For an instant I catch a glimpse of a bruise between her breasts, but it's hidden when she straightens. Her smiling image slides away as the lift opens and she steps inside.

'I'll be with you in ten minutes, crowds permitting,' she says.

'But I haven't told you—'

'Oh my God, try not to be such a provincial hick when we're seen together. My plant gave me your locale soon as we linked.'

I can't see her face anymore; just fingers drumming nervously on the handrail of the lift, its dim interior strobing due to a faulty light source. When she speaks again, her voice is at odds with the uneasy movement of her hand.

'I'm assuming by the look of that hideous can you're standing in, that you need me to take you shopping? See you shortly, darling. Prepare yourself for a spending. I won't be happy till you've joined the rest of us poor bastards in debt hell.'

The link goes dark. I smile at nothing in particular. It just feels good to be here at last; feels good to be waiting for Bel. Only … something is tainted. I don't know what. Probably just the awkwardness of our long separation; my anxiety at being here; nothing. But I'm left uneasy.

'How are my two best prod-liners?'

Jakel, head of department, leans over the production bench and grins, flashing his enhanced incisors. He makes my skin itch and my insides curl away in disgust. Bel says I should learn to be more sophisticated: deviants are commonplace in the cities now. If Jakel wants to live out his fantasy biting people and sucking on a bit of blood, good luck to him. There are plenty out there who enjoy being bitten.

Bel got me the job in Implant. She's in Sales, and I'm just an assembler, so our paths rarely cross at work. I'm partnered with Amai: small, quiet, and intelligent, with quick hands. She makes me look clumsy in comparison, and is often rectifying my mistakes. I like her. She doesn't speak of her past and I don't ask but, from things she's let slip, I get the impression she's no stranger to the slum rings. Maybe as a consequence of her poor background, or maybe from choice, she, like me, is free from enhancements – except, of course, for her com-link. All firm employees are given the basic model free of charge. The pressure on me to be fitted was unrelenting and almost cost me my job. Out of desperation, I feigned a reluctant confession to purity as a deviance – who knows, maybe it is – and this was accepted. My case was helped by Jakel, who all too eagerly championed my cause. Unfortunately, it means I have to put up with his "special attention".

Jakel circles our bench and, with a hand on each of our shoulders, draws Amai and me together so we can both feel the pressure of his hips and groin on our backs.

'My beautiful Pures,' he breathes. 'When are one of you lovelies going to give me a little taste?'

Amai curls in on herself, hunching over the bench; it's how she deals with Jakel's advances. I'm made from different stuff. I jab my elbow into his groin and turn to confront the pointy-toothed twat. I also figure, if I draw his attention, he'll leave my friend alone.

'Go screw yourself,' I say, and give him an engaging smile.

Jakel straightens up and forces a grin. 'The more you resist, Laina, the sweeter your juice,' he says. 'Come on, just a drop.' He pulls a long pin from his lapel. 'Give me a little suck on your pinkie.'

'I think the lady said to go pleasure yourself.' Bel's sudden appearance is welcome. She leans on her knuckles over the bench, her presence, as always, a threat and an invite: a heady mix of sexual muskiness and adrenaline. Her tail whips from side to side like a seriously pissed-off cat.

'I shall,' he says. 'A great deal of pleasure – you would

know if you synched with me.' He stalks away, rubbing his crotch and licking his incisors.

'God, what a pathetic little turd!' Bel plucks the manipulators from my hand. 'Come on; shift whistle's about to blow. Let's get out of here.'

A short, shrill sound transforms the focussed atmosphere of the prod room in an instant. Suddenly, there's chatter and movement as the shift changes. I gather up my tools. The worker who takes over my station is enhanced and needs a whole different set of apparatus to do the same job. Amai has already gone; I catch a glimpse of her hurrying through to the changing pods.

'She didn't say goodbye.' I watch her slim figure till she's lost in the crowds.

'Don't think your little friend likes me,' says Bel, regarding me intensely. She smiles and resumes her normal flippant air. 'Shame, she's cute – wouldn't mind getting to know her better. P'raps we could have a threesome sometime?'

'Jesu, Bel, it was that suggestion that freaked her out!'

'Was it? Don't remember.'

Bel slips her tail round my thigh as we head for the exit.

'Oh well, can't have them all,' she says with a sigh. 'Come, my pretty Pure. Your turn to choose where we eat tonight.'

I wake, limbs jumbled with Bel's. The tip of her tail, inert and heavy, is coiled between my breasts and I wonder, not for the first time, how she afforded it. The dark skin of it is living tissue, seeded from her own DNA, grown through and meshed with the titanium skeleton and sensory circuitry of the plant. I run my finger along its smooth length and it shudders and tenses at my touch. The tip uncurls, questing for my nipple. There's a glint from beneath Bel's thick lashes, and a slow smile spreads across her face. I knock her tail away impatiently.

'What?' she says. 'You started it!' She stretches, yawning,

more feline than human.

'Was just wondering how the hell you paid for this thing.'

Bel's face falls, colour draining.

'Oh Bel, what do you owe?'

Her dark eyes regard me with such sorrow that I'm unable to speak. She strokes my cheek softly, lightly, and with a tenderness that tightens my heart.

'Too much ...'

She kisses me with the same dark concentration as her stare, and we make love with a ferocious passion I've never experienced with her before. Afterward, groggy and stupefied, there's no time for more questions as the alarm sounds.

The bed sinks into the floor, leaving us sprawling and laughing as the hygiene unit swings out of the wall. My habitation space has been transformed, mostly due to Bel, although, if I'd followed all of her advice, I would be in debt myself now. As it is, the bed is the only new purchase. The hygiene and cooking units were recommissioned, and the entertainment wall was a second-hand private sale. It has a few glitches but is good enough. I switch it to live feed from the exterior and the city flickers into view. The outside camera is from a high vantage point. I haven't worked out where my room is in relation to the exterior but, whenever I turn on the feed, I experience a moment of disorientation, so I figure the two don't correspond. The sun hasn't broken through the heavy atmosphere - it rarely does - and the city lights strobe and glow in the smog. It looks like a fine acid drizzle has started as, down below, tiny figures hurry along beneath protective shielding that buzzes a faint blue with the moisture.

I feel closer to Bel than I ever have, more so than in the days of our innocence, when we would run from our families and camp on the reservations for days at a time. Something about the raw honesty of her despair, and the potency of our lovemaking this morning, makes me feel I have touched the real Bel for the first time. We're as stupid and fond as new lovers, all the way into the heart of the city and the huge Implant building. In the echoing temple of the vast lobby, we kiss with open warmth, before parting for the day's work, taking separate elevators, up and down. I don't realise how precious that last soft touch and fleeting view of her face, happy and unguarded, will become.

Late to my workstation, I'm surprised to see the bench empty: Amai isn't in.

'You're late for the third time this month; if it happens again, I'll have to dock your credits.' Jakel brushes past. 'And now it looks like your bad habits are rubbing off on your little friend. If she's not here in the next quarter, personnel will have to be told. Unauthorised absence can mean dismissal. If you know where she is, tell her to get her bony arse here quick.'

I slip my com from my overalls and, keeping it out of view under the bench, try to contact Amai. There's no response, just static. I can't understand it; her implant is new and, if there was a malfunction, it would go to a central message. It's just dead. I keep trying for the next half hour – nothing. Jakel keeps glancing over. He looks increasingly pissed off. After nearly an hour, he's back at my bench, his face creased in a frown.

'Where the hell is she?' he hisses. 'I've left it as long as I dare. I'll be in trouble as it is for not reporting her absence yet.'

'I don't know. Her com-link's dead.'

'No shit!' He chews on a fingernail, staring at the doors as if willing her to appear. 'Can't stall anymore. I'll try and fudge it; say she was feeling sick yesterday.'

'Hey, Jakel,' I call after him, as he walks away. 'Thanks. You're not such an arsehole after all.'

'Does that mean I'll get a little suck for lunch?'

I give him the finger, but not in the way he's expecting.

'There's gratitude!' he calls back.

As he crosses the room his face takes on the abstracted look of someone using their communication implant, but I can read the nuances of his expressions; he's not good at hiding them. Sly charm quickly dissolves, and his body tenses: he's worried – no, afraid. He avoids me for the rest of the morning. Amai doesn't arrive. After lunch, someone new has replaced her.

In the lobby, after work, Bel's deep in conversation with a suited man. She looks angry. He looks confident, condescending, sleek and well paid: a man used to power. They break off when they see me, and he slips away in the crowded space. Bel puts on a bright smile.

'Darling Pretty,' she calls, 'where to tonight? No wait, it's my turn. I know just the thing – decadent as hell. Shit, it makes hell look like a convent, but the food's—'

'Amai's missing.'

'Who?'

'Don't – you know who – the girl I work with. She's gone. Her com's dead. Jakel won't tell me anything. I know he knows something. He's avoiding me, and she's been replaced already; some lad – he barely speaks – but I don't think he knows anything … don't think he's involved—'

'*Involved?* What are you jabbering about? You're making it sound like she's been spirited away! People leave all the time; there's no mystery. This is the city, darling!'

'She wouldn't have gone without saying something … saying goodbye …'

'Like last night?'

I don't have an answer, but it doesn't feel right. Bel has already changed the subject, is chatting happily again, about food, sex, office gossip; I don't know, I'm not listening. Her flippancy is irritating.

'Laina, are you coming?'

We're outside. The copper-and-glass doors thud and pop as they revolve behind us.

'No, you go ahead. I'm done in. Just want an early night,' I say.

Anger darkens Bel's features: it's her go-to emotion to mask pain. 'Your loss.' She stalks off, tail swishing.

The intimacy of this morning feels irretrievable. I hesitate. I don't know what to do. I'm suddenly lost. I wanted Bel to go away but, beyond that, I hadn't thought any further. I don't want to go home. I stare at the seething crowds. As usual, the city is a mass of movement, so it's the stillness that attracts my attention: a small figure across the street is watching the building intently – a girl. There's something familiar about her.

Crossing directly is impossible: the automated traffic is too fast and too dense. I'll have to take the underpass. The girl is still immobile, focussed on the doors behind me. I consider attracting her attention, to get her to wait, but don't want to spook her. The subway is close but the crush of commuters is at a virtual standstill, squashed into the bottleneck of an entrance. I shove and trample through, ignoring the protests and insults. I hate these tunnels at the best of times and avoid them if I can. My chest tightens and black spots swim in front of my eyes. The press of humanity is claustrophobic. I emerge, sweating and gasping for air, and have to wait for my vision to clear. The girl is gone. Shit.

She had been standing at the top of a flight of steps that once gave access to the road. Wire fencing has been put up to try and dissuade anyone stupid enough to contemplate crossing the traffic. It was the perfect vantage point to observe the entrance to Implant. I'm staring across the street, unsure what to do, how to find her, when the hairs on the back of my neck prickle: someone's watching me. I turn and scan the crowd. Most people have their heads down. No one is looking my way. There are no windows at street level, and those higher up are one-way mirror glass; impossible to tell if I'm being observed from anywhere in there. Along the street is a break between the buildings: a narrow service alley. A slight movement catches my eye. Ah …

The passage is dark, barely the width of two people. Ducts and pipes pepper the walls, making it seem an even tighter space. Both buildings are at least twenty stories and the light is fading anyway so, further in, away from the illumination of the street, it looks pitch-black. I feel my way in the gloom. The place is thick with refuse. I slip on something slimy and swear under my breath. Something scurries over my foot and I bite back a scream. The sound of the street gradually fades behind the hum of vents and maintenance machinery. In the dim light, I can see a set of metal doors in one of the walls and, in the recess, a shadowy figure.

'Hello,' I say. 'I won't hurt you.'

The girl steps out but keeps her distance, alert and guarded. She looks about twelve, small and thin, and is dressed in worn, faded clothes. Her jacket is too large; maybe a hand-me-down she hasn't grown into yet; maybe all she can get. She's clean though and someone has made an effort to mend and patch her coveralls – so, poor but not destitute.

'Are you Laina?' She says, shifting nervously. Everything about her is tense, ready to run. Then it dawns on me why she's so familiar.

'You're Amai's …'

'Sister.'

'Of course, she never really speaks about home, but I'm sure she mentioned you—'

'You're Laina?'

'Yes.'

'She speaks of you often. Where is she? What's happened? Please …' The girl's voice falters, and I can see she's fighting back tears. My stomach knots.

'I don't know; I've been trying her com all day.'

'It's dead. Been that way since last night,' the girl says. 'I spoke to her when she finished shift; said she'd been called into Fitting to have her three-month service. When she wasn't home by ten, I tried the link and just got static. I begged her not to get the link, but she said she'd lose her job without it.'

'What's wrong with having a link?'

The girl hesitates, and gives me an appraising look. She clearly doesn't trust me.

'Have heard rumours, that's all … it's nothing. They won't let me into the building. Can you ask in Fitting if they saw her?'

'Sure, I'll go now. Can you wait here?'

'Not safe, curfew nearly down and I have to be back in the outer ring. Will you come there?'

'Yes.'

'I'll wait at checkpoint nine. Be careful, Laina.'

She slips out of the alley, and melts into the crowd. I'm left uneasy. My stomach churns, and I realise I never asked her name.

It takes some persuading to get back into Implant: workers don't usually want to return after shift. I convince security that I've finally plucked up the courage to talk to Fitting about a com-link, and if I don't do it now I never will. I'm known throughout the company as Liana the Pure, so my change of heart is a matter of immense delight. The guards enjoy taking the piss before they let me pass.

Fitting is in sub-basement three. The manufacturing floors are operational twenty-four seven, but everywhere else is office hours only, so it's strangely quiet when the lift doors open. Security checked, so I know there will be someone in the department, but the corridor is empty and silent, except for the soft hum of generators. Frosted glass doors at the far end show bright lights beyond. My mouth is dry and my palms sweaty. This is stupid. I've let the girl spook me. I just need to ask if they've seen Amai, and if she mentioned where she was going afterwards. No big deal. I step out of the lift and a man suddenly emerges from a side door dragging a cart laden with cleaning stuff.

'Oh,' I say, trying to stop my heart racing, 'didn't know the company had cleaners.'

'Automation system's bust. Got me in last week. S'pect they'll boot me out soon as it's fixed. Sorry if I gave you a fright.'

I mumble, 'okay,' and sidle past.

As I'm half way down the corridor, he speaks again. 'Gave the other one a fright last night … seems folk ain't used to seein' people do honest work no more.'

'Other one?'

'Yesterday, 'bout this time. Young like you, but not so pretty.' The man leers at me but, when I don't respond, he continues: 'Sweet girl; took the time to chat. Said she was here for a service. I said—'

I hold up my old com-link to show him a picture of Amai.

'Aye, that's the lass. Nice girl.'

Thanking him, I head for the glass doors. So she was definitely here. I feel less jumpy; maybe she said something in Fitting about where she was headed next.

As I reach out for the palm-panel to open the door, the man speaks again. 'Watch yourself in there,' he says, and trundles into another office along the corridor.

The frosted doors of Fitting slide open. A Tech is sitting at a broad desk reading through some papers. He looks up and, for a fleeting moment, a look of surprise, almost panic, flits across his face. 'The department's closed,' he says, and shuffles the jumble of papers into a file.

Something about his manner, and the warnings I've

had, make me cautious. I decide to stick to the story I've given security. So, with a broad smile, I introduce myself and stride forward as if to shake his hand, hoping to get a look at the name on the file. It's slid into a drawer before I can get near enough. He doesn't return my smile or take my proffered hand.

'We're closed. Contact the department Monday and make an appointment.'

I stumble through the story, but he doesn't look like he's buying it. I'm starting to sweat. Oh, well, here goes nothing … 'I've been dead set against having an implant, till my friend had one a few months ago. She's been raving about how brilliant it is. So, I'm persuaded! You probably remember her; she was down here last night for her three-month service … Amai – Amai Torvald?'

'The department was closed last night, and we don't do a service unless something malfunctions.'

'Oh! I'm sure she came. It was after shift – about seven?'

'You're mistaken. The department was closed at five yesterday, same as every day. No one was here.'

My stomach tightens and the hairs prickle on my neck. I need to get out. Gabbling an apology and promises to call after the weekend, I retreat back through the doors, thanking him for his time. The Tech remains immobile and silent, watching me leave. Just before the doors hiss shut, I hear him speak; I don't know if it's a com-link, or whether someone else is in the room; someone I hadn't noticed. 'We may have a problem,' he says.

The doors click locked. The thick glass prevents me from hearing any more. As I hurry to the lifts, I keep checking over my shoulder, not looking where I'm going, and crash into the cleaner.

'Steady!'

'Sorry!'

'That was quick! You're out sooner than the other lassie.'

'You saw her leave then?' Relief floods through me – this has been a misunderstanding after all. I've let my imagination run riot. What a tit! Bel's going to piss herself laughing when I tell her.

'No, that's not what I'm sayin'. She didn't come out; not while I was here anyways.'

My heart misses a beat. I jab at the lift call; I've got to get out. The walls are closing in.

The cleaner must have noticed my face fall, because his tone's apologetic when he speaks again. 'I was here till just gone ten … no one came out, but the light was still on down there. Maybe she—'

I don't wait to hear any more; the lift opens and I stumble inside. Along the corridor, the frosted doors click and hiss open. Frantic, I thump the lift buttons, keeping my eyes on the bright space beyond the glass. No one emerges, but I can't breathe until the lift closes and I'm ascending to the lobby. God, what am I getting myself into?

I've never been into the outer rings – the industrial districts; the slums. I know checkpoint nine though: most of the clubs Bel has taken me to are close to the checkpoints; places on the edge in every sense. I wish she was with me; I'm afraid. Her lust for life always dispels the darkness, always has. I've tried linking, but it went straight to message. She must still be mad. I haven't tried again. I'm worried about the stuff Amai's sister said; worried they'll trace me through the com and listen in on the conversation. Who "they" are, I don't know – if they *are* anyone! I'm getting paranoid. Get a grip!

Even though it's late, I don't have any trouble at the checkpoint; questions are rarely asked. Inhabitants of the inner ring often seek distraction, adventure, a bit of rough: drugs, or maybe even try and do some good in the slums. The guard scans my identity tattoo and waves me through with barely a glance. Holo-sport is on a monitor in the cabin, and he hurries back as his colleague whoops at a score.

The most noticeable difference beyond the checkpoint is the dark. The inner ring is ablaze day and night, a glittering jewel of commerce and consumption. Here, energy is precious, limited.

Light-headed, legs shaking, afraid and alone, I walk into the night-black streets. The girl isn't here. What if she doesn't come? The streets are narrow, convoluted, filled with filth. My head spins. Figures bump me in the gloom, shadowy figures I can't see. The world spins. I graze my cheek on a wall. Darkness. Spinning. 'Catch her,' someone calls. No! I lash out and fall.

'Laina … Laina, it's okay. You're okay.'

I stop struggling and blink to adjust my eyes to the light; it seems very bright. Then a face comes into focus: Aima's sister. I relax.

'You passed out – sorry I wasn't at the gate – lucky I found you. We're at a friend's house.'

A man's profile swims into view. He turns and smiles, passes me a glass of water. I sit up gingerly and take a sip. The world is still tilting.

'When did you last eat?' he asks.

'This morning.'

He grunts and leaves the room. I tell the girl about Fitting and, before I finish, he's back with a cup of broth.

'It's a bad idea to go poking around there: those people are dangerous,' he says. 'Hanah, why did you let her do this?'

So, her name's Hanah. I swallow some of the broth and immediately feel a little better.

'I shouldn't have asked you to go. I'm sorry,' she says.

'What are you talking about? How are they dangerous? It's ridiculous!' I laugh. Now that I'm safe, the whole episode seems foolish.

'There are rumours,' the man says. He isn't smiling. 'People go missing.'

'Oh, come on …'

'You know that, to fit an implant, they have to make space …' He taps his head. '… in here.'

'Of course. It's perfectly safe,' I say, but it's one of the reasons I'm reluctant to have the procedure.

'Safe?'

'There are risks, sure …'

'It goes wrong more than you'd believe – more than they'll let on – more than it should.'

'Where are all the casualties then? What happens to them? We would know.'

'They're careful who they choose. Those without connections or family; people who won't be missed; the ones no one cares about; the poor.'

'Well that proves your theory is bullshit – Amai has family.'

'Did she ever speak of me at work?' says Hanah. 'Does the company even know about me?'

'Well …'

'I told her it was stupid, that she wasn't protecting me, just putting herself at risk. Oh, Amai, why didn't you listen?'

Hanah bolts from the room. I stare at the man in shock. 'What do you think's happened to Amai?'

'Sold.'

I laugh. 'What, to the body snatchers?'

'She wasn't dead – not technically. The slave trade is booming.'

I'm not laughing now. My skin prickles. I can taste the broth in my throat.

'People go in willingly to have the plant and, when the bastards are in here …' He taps his head again. '… making space, the person gets erased: memories, personality, everything that makes them who they are. Then the living husk is sold – as a sex slave, a chem-worker, a punch bag, a wife – whatever you've ordered, those boys in Fitting will find you a match.'

'Absurd! You're insane!' I can't believe I'm listening to this crap.

'You need to be careful, lady: I hear collectors out there pay big money for a Pure like you.'

Hanah is back in the doorway, leaning heavily on the frame, her face ashen.

'This is shit, Hanah. I'll find Amai, I promise.'

Back out on the street, I hear the man call from inside, '*Big* money!'

Once I'm through the checkpoint, I risk linking Bel again. I really need to see her, be enveloped in her warmth; enjoy her take on the absurdity of tonight. She answers.

'Hey.'

'Hey yerself.'

There's no vis and I hear a man's voice: 'That her?' I know Bel isn't exclusive to me. I don't see her for days, sometimes weeks at a time, but to hear the evidence unsettles me.

'Sorry, you're busy,' I mumble.

'It was you blew *me* out, remember? What's up? You sound weird.'

'Yeah, it's been a weird night!'

'Tell your Aunty Bel all about it then.'

'Not over the com; I've heard some stuff and … well, I'm not sure linking is safe. Can we talk face to face?'

'Darling, if you want to see me, you just have to say; not go all cloak and dagger. Rene's will just be getting lively about now. Meet me there, half an hour.'

The link goes dead. I breathe easily, a weight lifted. Bel is going to find my adventure hilarious, and you can bet she won't let me forget how gullible I've been for a long time to come.

Rene's Bar is a dive in the twisted alleys behind Implant. Bel was right: even though it's gone midnight, the place is only just getting going. I squeeze into the sweaty crowd, wondering how I'll find her in the press of bodies. The place pulses with the buzz of hedonistic pleasure, jacked into the rising tempo of the music. Something warm coils around my waist: Bel's tail. She draws me through the mass of throbbing bodies to the booths at the back of the room.

'Hey Dougie, how you been?' Bel addresses a rangy man with tiger stripes and unusually green eyes, who's lounging in one of the booths. 'How 'bout you scram so I can have a clandestine chat with my little friend here? I'll owe you.'

'The usual?'

'Don't you ever get tired of it?'

'Not with you.'

'How 'bout I throw in …' she leans forward and whispers in his ear. His eyes go wide and he grins.

'I'll get Rene to send over drinks for that!' He gives me a wink as he slides out to let us in.

High padded seats muffle the sounds of the bar. I suddenly feel tense, unsure of what to say, how to begin. Bel chats about the clientele - who's doing who; who *wants* to do who - until our drinks arrive and I launch into the evening's events. By the time I've finished, she's laughing so hard, tears are streaming down her face.

'Oh my poor baby!' She crushes me in a hug. 'What a time you've had.' Throwing back her head, she roars again. 'Wish I'd been there! Oh, I know: let's break into Fitting and get a look at that mysterious folder?'

'Yeah, ha ha, laugh it up.'

'I'm deadly serious.'

Bel isn't laughing anymore; she's staring at me intently.

'It would be madness!'

'The perfect end to your crazy adventure … come on, let's do it!'

'And impossible—'

'Maybe not … I know the codes for the back entrance, and we're not going to steal anything, so it's not really breaking and entering. Say yes.'

'It's insane …' But I've promised to find Amai, and whatever's in that file may be my only lead. What the hell … don't have a better plan!

The basement levels are deserted, the silence eerie; just the low hum of the generators. I can't stop giggling. This is so ludicrous. We make it to the corridor outside Fitting without being challenged. It's in darkness.

'Your turn,' says Bel. 'Are you still any good at picking locks?'

'There's much to recommend a misspent youth.' I smile at her, and have to control another wave of hysteria before getting started on the door panel.

It takes me a while; locks have changed since I was a kid. Eventually there's a satisfying click and, with a hiss, the door slides open. 'Ta da …'

Bel pulls me into a tight embrace and a passionate kiss. After a while, I pull away. 'Not exactly the time and place!'

'Always the time and place for you,' she says, smiling, but her voice is heavy with sadness.

I don't have time for one of her mood swings, as I'm worried I've triggered an alarm. Hurrying round the desk, I try the drawer; it isn't locked. The top file has Amai's name on it.

'Found it!' I grin, but Bel's frowning at something behind me. A sharp sting burns the back of my neck, and I can't move: *paralysed!*

Bel turns away. *What?* The tech from earlier walks out from behind me and joins her in the doorway. I struggle to shout, get Bel's attention, but I can't speak. *This isn't happening!*

'Bit late for a call,' he says. 'In future, I'd rather arrange delivery with more notice.'

'Had to be now … you know why.' Bel's voice is flat, emotionless.

Please turn around. The joke's gone far enough! Please turn around!

'Are we all square?' says Bel. She still won't look at me.

'For this one?' The tech glances over. 'Sure, you're all paid up … till you want the next implant …' He laughs.

I can see Bel's profile: her jaw is clenched. *Bel, you're frightening me!* She walks away.

Oh God, Bel, please come back. You bloody selfish bitch, please …

Another tech arrives, and they lift me into the back room. *Bel …* I can't move or speak; I can breathe – barely – and blink, and that's it. *Bel, don't leave me!*

'Are we fitting this one with anything?' It's the tech I haven't seen before.

'No, this one's for The Collector; he said any Pures are for him, any price, but they have to be unadulterated. This one's perfect. He'll pay a fortune.'

'We not erasing her then?'

'Course we are! Everything has to go. He's very particular: memories, personality, the lot – she has to be wiped clean.'

This can't be happening! Bel, you bitch, walk back in, help me for fu—

They're strapping something around my head; attaching electrodes to my temples. *Please, God don't!*

'What's he do with them?'

'He's started some kind of breeding programme.'

'Yeah, right! Dirty bugger.' They both laugh.

Laugh! She'll kick your arse for that … Bel …

'He's trying to keep the Pure line untainted. Thinks he's saving humanity. Councillor Fraike: saviour of the human race!'

My uncle! This is a mistake; he's my uncle. For God's sake, you've made a mistake. You have to stop! It's a mistake!

'Put something between her teeth; don't want her biting half her tongue off.'

Get off, you bastards. This is a mistake! Bel—

Something clicks; there's a buzzing in my head.

Bel … BelpleasepleaseGodhelp me … please … help … m—

THE WELL–DECEIVED

By Joanna Richardson

'So, as you can see,' Dr Shleiner intones, 'the new neurons demonstrate a complete arborisation - that is, they have a good amount of new connections with themselves and the surviving neurons. It's a great integration; more than we expected.'

'Terrific,' I mutter, probably not sounding as enthused as I should.

'Of course,' she continues, sounding slightly bashful, 'your connectome is obviously not the same as it was.'

'Of course,' I agree, vaguely.

Earlier, she had been saying something about how I was lucky, because I still had a "skeleton" of neural pathways remaining after my illness, with no area completely destroyed, but I had got lost ages ago. She zooms out, so that I can see an overview of the whole thing: a dizzying mass of shaded wires that split into infinitely finer strands, invisible at this magnification. Helpfully, the display flashes red for the old version of my brain, and green for the new one. A swell of nausea roils up in my stomach, as if it is protesting against its fellow organ.

'Well anyway, that's great,' I say hastily, pulling the VR goggles off and forestalling hearing more stuff I don't want to hear, and wouldn't understand if I did. Besides, I think I have just made myself seasick looking at my own brain.

Back in the garden, Gareth is describing his latest hallucination for the group, although, as usual, it's a performance for the doctors as much as anything. Something about going into the garden and finding a flower blooming. His mother was inside, performing some sort of improbable sex act with a bee. Anyway, I tuned out as soon as I saw where this one was leading. It's difficult to know if he fools the psychiatrist or not; she has that typical shrink aura of secret knowing, which always feels like revealed wisdom when you hear it at the time and, when you try to recall it later, just sounds like trite rubbish. Gary's faux-Freudian fantasies are always bullshit, and I can't believe she doesn't see that at least. It's not that I don't believe he hallucinates - I *know* he does - I just don't believe he ever sees what he says he sees. I always drift off, wondering why he lies. If *I* were the doctor, I'd find the more interesting question.

So I ask him, as we walk slowly around the garden afterwards, but he only grins and evades me too.

'Because it's fun.'

'That's no answer.'

'All right. Why should I tell *them* what I see?'

'Well, for one thing, if you told the truth, then you might get something out of these sessions.'

He snorts derisively at that, and I can't blame him. I don't even know why I said it.

We have our own little sub-group, Gary, Janice and I (well, and Theo, sort of, although he's been bounced back to the main hospital). The "*This is a pointless waste of time*" sub-group.

'Aren't you going to ask me what I really see?'

'No,' I say, after some consideration. 'You'd probably lie to me too. And anyway, it's *your* mind.'

'That's just it,' he says, with dry irony; 'it's *not* my mind, just like it's not his leg.' He nods in the direction of Amir, making his way slowly past the rose bushes with his odd, crab-legged gait, and the strange expression of someone who is trying really hard to pretend something isn't happening right next to them.

'How can you end up thinking you have an extra leg anyway?' I wonder.

'Same way you can end up thinking you have an extra personality?' Gary suggests, and I know he is referring to Theo (or rather, *not* Theo). Then he switches the topic abruptly to me. 'Still having your weird beach memory?'

I frown, annoyed. 'Yes.'

'Work out where it's come from yet?'

I glance at him sidelong. Now it's my turn to smile wryly. For all I know, it's not *my* weird beach memory, after all. 'Honestly, I'm beginning to think I just made it up.'

In the afternoon, I have the usual photo session with my wife. All in all, I'd rather be in therapy. Our slideshow today is Berlin, 2032. It's slightly more interesting this time, because I've never seen this one before, but there are fewer videos, because we didn't have Maria then. Aisha had always preferred snapshots over video anyway; she was never one to document every second of our holidays and blog it all up, let alone our everyday lives; neither was I. I preferred to live in the moment and take the memories (apparently). But my memories are gone, and I know that Aisha roundly curses having not taken more videos, or writing more blogs. Mostly, what we have left is from holidays, so she has to work from that. We went through all the family stuff ages ago – a small mercy.

'Anything look familiar?' she asks, with the dull hopelessness of someone who's heard "No" far too often.

'No,' I say, and don't tell her that I can't remember ever going to Berlin at all. Berlin, Paris, New York; the list of unforgettable cities I've forgotten visiting is embarrassingly large. We'll have Berlin again in a few days, see if it has jogged anything loose. I know from the past few months of doing this that all I'll remember is watching a slideshow today of the time we went to Berlin. 'I remember when you had your hair like that though,' I say, in an effort to appease, because Aisha looks upset, and I hate upsetting her.

'I had it like that for four years, Art,' she says, exasperated.

So I've said the wrong thing again. Her hair is white now. She could change that but she doesn't want to, and I don't want her to either. It's the way I've always remembered it, even if that is for less than three years.

My gaze drifts around the room as she carries grimly on. I can't help it. I'm sick of this. The walls are filled with overloaded bookshelves; there are piles of books all over the table too, dirty mugs and saucers perched precariously around them, a wispy discarded scarf of Aisha's, some mail. I remember, when I first started getting my cognition back properly, spending hours browsing all those old-new books, so enticing and exotic; like whole new countries to explore, filled with stories, art, and history. Like Berlin must have been when we went on holiday there.

Aisha had been delighted at my progress to start with; far beyond her wildest hopes. I'd been brought back from a wild, animal-like state, forever frightened and irrational, to a civilised, thinking human being, one whose sentences made sense again; someone who could do something one day and not forget it the next. Gary asked me once if I remembered what it was like being like that, but I didn't give him an answer. He can keep what he sees to himself, and I can keep what it's like being subhuman to myself. Mostly I remember the confusion, and the fear. People aren't meant to exist like that; terrified creatures caught in the trap of their own dim self-awareness that they should be, and once were, *more*.

The books on the table are for her history studies. Aisha's clever, and brilliant at history; less so at science (not that Dr Shleiner would give me very good marks for that myself). Mostly though, I think she doesn't *want* to understand the doctors. She wants to believe I'm like those cases of amnesia, that if she only prods me enough with photographs and stories of my life, then all my memories will come flooding back. I've tried to explain to her myself that dementia doesn't work like that; that all those brain cells, with all their complicated little connections, just died, and took the memories with them. You can't resurrect the dead, or their memories. And no matter how they tried to reassure with their talk of *topographic dendritic maps* (taken from my pre-Alzheimer's scans), of their re-arborisation, their *neural reinforcement* and *stem cells this and that*, they couldn't have seriously believed that what would grow back would be exactly the same as before. And neither could Aisha. I don't understand why she persists in the face of her own common sense.

The first support group they put me in was for amnesiacs. Like a long round of pin the tail on the donkey that was, with blind minds trying to stab out and randomly hit buried memories. Awful. I left after the first session and never came back. So they stuck me with the others, because they don't have Alzheimer's cases like me anymore (well, mixed dementia technically, I think). Nobody gets that far gone anymore; not so bad that even most of the long-term, episodic memory goes. I was the worst they had ever seen. There are several papers on me – Patient D.

I hear Aisha sometimes, talking to her sister on the phone. At the start she was wildly optimistic. It was all "it only took him a week to learn how to button his shirt", and "he recognised the new doctor", through to the dizzying heights of "he solved the crossword" and "we held a real conversation for the first time in I don't know how long, and he really understood it this time". Later though, it was all sobbing and "he's not the same anymore; he's back to normal but he's not *Art*". There's less sobbing now, more rational assessment; more of "it's not like he's the same person he was before but, at the same time, it's still my Art, you know?

He still has the same personality, and all those funny little habits". I wish I knew what my funny little habits were. I'd do them more, if it made her happy. But it all comes down to one thing: "he still doesn't remember what he lost. And he lost so much. He doesn't remember any of it. Will he ever remember?".

In the evenings, I read late: old emails, things from friends, things we wrote each other, things from Maria … anything I can get my hands on. I want so desperately to fill the gaps for her. I'm not sure why; perhaps it's because I see how much she tries to fill the gaps for me; or maybe it's for all those years of love that morphed into something unrecognisable, just as I did, and came back altered, like me. Perhaps it's just empathy; I cannot stand to see her disappointment, her sadness. Or maybe it's my own odd sensations of not being quite all there. I *do* remember stuff; mostly older stuff. My own childhood, I recall quite well still; my own daughter's, less so and, somehow, that feels profoundly *wrong*. I guess the earlier successes in learning new things, the factual stuff, lent us both a false sense of security. They were the first things to go, so when they were so easy to relearn, it was easy to hope. But that's the thing: I *re-learnt* them, easily, with my new, data-hungry, brain-neurone-connectome-thingy. I didn't actually *remember* though.

I thought I remembered something I'd forgotten the other day. I'd been flush with excitement about telling her. It was when we were looking through the snaps of Yorkshire, and this image had just come to me, of walking along a stretch of sandy beach, and I'd blurted it out excitedly.

'Art, we didn't go to the beach in Yorkshire,' she said. 'We weren't anywhere near it.'

'Maybe it was from some other place, and this just reminded me,' I said, but I'd sounded doubtful even to myself.

'Well, do you remember if you were alone or by yourself?

How old were you? Was it hot, cold, rainy? Were there other people there? Ships on the sea?' The barrage of questions had unsettled me.

'I just remember a beach! A sandy beach. Just the beach,' I said, uselessly.

I'd brought it up a couple more times, just in case, but she'd gotten angry, so I'd stopped talking about it. Gary's right though: I do still remember it, often, and it *is* remembering, not just thinking about it. I wonder where it came from?

The brain regrowth trials were, by their very nature, more experimental than most initial human trials. They had to be; the monkey models they tested it on first could only show restored function. They can watch behaviour, of course, but monkeys can't talk. Monkeys can't say, "Well I feel better, but I don't remember a thing." But people are desperate, willing to try anything and, in many ways, it must have seemed like a miracle, the holy grail: to replace damaged human neural tissue. It was easiest at first for more modest damage; discrete areas affected by stroke were a big early success, but of course they got more ambitious the more successful they were until, before long, they were replacing whole chunks of damaged brains. When it worked so well for Parkinson's, they set their sights higher than enabling the lame and shaky to walk. Alzheimer's was always experimental; all the dementias were, really. They didn't know if what remained of the damaged brain would start making the new stuff diseased too, but of course then the protein engineering field was coming along in leaps and bounds since the second CJD epidemic had afflicted so many people, and they finally managed to make good prions that converted all the bad prions, or got rid of them.

Wish I'd got me some of those sooner, I think, regularly. They've refined all the techniques a lot now, and anyway, they can intervene before it gets really bad. Before you get anywhere near what I was like. There are still side-effects though, unintended consequences, particularly amongst the earlier human subjects. Like our little group.

Amir had been paralysed by a stroke; only, when his brain grew back, it got itself confused and now he has some weird opposite of phantom limb syndrome: his brain thinks it's got an extra leg that isn't even there. Janice was a vCJD victim, nearly as full of holes in her head as I was; they thought the brain regrowth had been essentially random, and left her completely insane (not unknown), so much did she stagger and scream and start at loud sounds, making no sense to anybody. But she's sane, except that she has synaesthesia. Half her senses re-wired themselves. She's probably doing better than the rest of us; she's adapting. She was a news anchor before, but she cannot take the complicated sensory chaos of a studio now. She likes quiet places with muted colours, but she's getting better and she's making the most amazing art. I wish I'd turned out with a brand new talent to go with the brand new me, instead of trading one nondescript guy for another. I wish I could remember something more from those gaps.

Theo is back at the session the following week, much improved, and he joins Gary and I on our little scornful walk around the gardens. Last week he had some sort of breakdown and was now almost as crazy as Janice had been. Amir is sitting on a bench staring at the ground; Janice is staring enraptured at a tree -I know that she is listening to the soft whisper of the leaves and seeing stars in her mind, and I guiltily envy her.

'How's your other half?' Gary asks Theo, which pisses Theo off.

'You know perfectly well Jed left me months ago.'

'He doesn't mean *that* other half,' I say, before an argument breaks out; Gary's insistent need on stirring things up.

'Oh, you mean Ziggy.'

'You gave it a name now?' Gary asks, fascinated in spite of himself.

'It's not an *it*, it's a *him*. I called him Ziggy after Bowie's alter ego. My Grandma was a massive fan.'

For some reason, Gary finds this funny and laughs. I don't. I don't know who Bowie is. Somebody famous, I guess, or once was.

'I thought extra personalities sort of came with their own names already,' Gary says, and I know he is genuinely curious.

Gary used to be schizophrenic (or so he says); *really* delusional. I don't know what they did to him, and he still won't tell us, but if he's still seeing stuff that isn't there, it can't have worked that well. Besides, he was probably always weird. I wonder whether the old me would have tolerated him quite so well as I do, then wonder whether that wishful thinking indicates some sort of desire that I have been not only *restored*, but also *improved*. When I come out of my brief musing, Theo's already answered and I've missed it.

'I thought you switched between the two personalities and don't remember what the other one did,' I say, trying to re-engage.

'It's not that simple.'

Nothing ever is, is it?

I have two more months of the support group before I give up and chuck it in, although our subgroup keep in touch. During that time, I manage to have a ferocious argument with Aisha. I got fed up with the slideshows, then one day I saw that she'd left her computer on with the next one open. I cheated and peeked ahead at Venice and pretended like I remembered loads of stuff. Needless to say, she totally caught me out. All it took were a couple of follow-up questions and I was lost at sea again. After that, things became cool between us, but she finally stops with the shows, which is a relief.

Janice invites me to her first exhibition; a smallish affair but, apparently, known as a jumping-off point for a number of successful artists, which I understand to mean it's a Big Deal. So I go along. Gary is there too, and it's obvious when I see them standing close together, laughing over their drinks, that they've had a more fruitful couple of months than I have. I'm surprised by how glad it makes me. Janice has moved on from painting to holographic sculpture, and the results are *astounding*. They come over to me as I'm staring at a particularly compelling piece. The old-fashioned print label underneath informs me that it is called *HEARING VOICES No.12*, which creates a suspicion in me.

'Gary and I have been collaborating,' Janice informs me, with that sly, knowing smile.

'I've become a *muse*,' Gary says, with an absurdly gleeful pride that is somehow terribly endearing, his arm around her waist. They seem so very young.

'I thought you had visual hallucinations,' I say, dryly.

Gary waves a hand and winks at me, mute.

'Well that depends how you look at it,' Janice answers for him, then spies Theo by the door, and skips excitedly off to see him before I can quiz her more.

'How's he doing?' I ask.

'Oh fine. They used some of that targeted gene therapy to make those nuisance extra neurons suicide, and now he doesn't have Ziggy anymore.'

'He's cured?' I ask, sceptically.

'Well, sort of. He told Janice the other day that there's this little remnant left. Just this little thing that gets happy and sad and frightened and isn't him. He says it's like having a pet dog in his head.'

'That's creepy,' I say, ghoulishly fascinated nonetheless. 'And Amir? Have you heard from him?'

'Don't you talk to people anymore, Art?'

'I heard something crazy about them doing a fake amputation,' I say, a little defensively.

Gary laughs. 'You're not far wrong. They came up with some scheme to make him think he was having his extra leg amputated - they used a model leg, and buckets of fake blood and everything - to fool his brain into believing it was gone. Of course, you know what happens then?'

'What?'

'He gets phantom limb syndrome. Or *phantom* phantom limb syndrome, if you like. Anyway, that's much easier to treat, so he's basically back to normal now.'

'Neuroscientists - they've got to be the craziest people out there,' I say.

'The science of the surreal,' Gary agrees, then asks, 'Aisha still mad at you?' For some reason, it's Gary I've chosen to confide in online. Perhaps it's because, underneath it all, he's very kind. Or perhaps it's because he's just so unlike me, and perhaps I only like that because I've forgotten what I *am* like. I can define myself by noticing how extraordinarily *not* Gary-like I am.

'Not really,' I say. 'I think she's just sort of resigned herself to things now.'

'Hmm. If you were going to lie,' Gary tells me, sounding more serious than his usual wont, 'you went about it the wrong way, my friend.' *Oh lord*, I suddenly think, *he's in love and now he thinks he can fix everybody else's relationships.* Why do people always do that?

'Well, what do you think I should have done?' I demand, a little testily.

'Look, forget the past ...' he begins, and I can't help it: I burst out laughing, long and hard.

'Forgetting the past is not the problem! It's *remembering* it, remember?'

That sets Gary off too, and for a few moments we're a little twosome of helpless giggles. Janice looks our way briefly, a dreamy smile on her face. I wonder what she sees.

'Look, I'm serious,' Gary says, when we finally catch our breath. 'What Aisha wants with you isn't a past; it's a *future*.'

'Then why does she keep dwelling on all these things I've forgotten?'

'Because she's scared that if you don't have anything of the past, then you've lost the foundations for the future.'

'Isn't she right?'

'No,' he says simply, 'because you've acted all along as if you have a future together, and you're the one who's forgotten most of the past you had with her. Just because you can't see the foundations, doesn't mean they're not there, in some way.'

He's right, of course, and I wonder why I never thought of it before; why the man who came back after the treatment didn't just say "But I don't know you", and walk away. But being with Aisha is as natural as breathing. I never question it.

'I don't see how this helps,' I say at last.

'Art, for every thousand things you've forgotten, she's forgotten at least ten; and your daughter, when she was small anyway, has forgotten more. Nobody remembers everything. You should use that. You don't need to remember all those things; you just need to create the *impression* of them being there. Like seeing a 3D image on a 2D screen.'

'I don't know that she'll fall for that,' I say doubtfully, still not sure what he means.

'As long as you're subtle, she'll believe it, because she wants to believe it. We are all of us self-deluded.'

That last is said in a slightly melancholy tone, and I look sharply at him, but he only gives that knowing smile, and swills his drink around coyly.

'Do you ever think that, when they promised to cure us," I say slowly, 'they never meant that they could restore us, only replace?'

'Or re-create,' he says, but I'm barely listening, because something he said has reminded me of something I thought I'd forgotten.

Then there's a gap, and it's later on, and I've had too much to drink, even more than Gary, and he's got my arm on one side, and Janice has the other; which is good, because my balance still goes if I'm really tired, and she's taking me over to a little piece in the corner that I haven't looked at, and saying, 'This one is for you, Art. We made it for you.' The blurry little label in front of it says *THE ART OF BEING WELL-DECEIVED*.

'That's a quote, isn't it?' I slur.

Janice's eyes widen in conspiratorial delight. 'You remember that?'

'I don't remember the rest of it, or who it's by, or where it's from though.'

'Well don't ask me, because I'm never going to tell you. It's perfect that that's all you remember.' I open my mouth to object, but she overrules me. 'You don't need it. You don't need it, Art.'

I look at the sculpture, and it almost makes my eyes hurt, the way there seems to be nothing there, but then there's layer upon layer: a hint of shadow here, a piece of light there. It reminds me of something too. I look at Janice and Gary together. Smiling. Knowing. Joyous in the new creation of themselves and each other, and I think, *I want that.* But I'm also thinking, *I mustn't forget that thing I just remembered.* And, *Lord, I'm drunk.*

It's late when I get back, and Aisha is already asleep. I drag up the last slideshow, the one that she would have given if I hadn't messed up. But memories aren't a slideshow; of course they're not. They're fragments, connected in the most unlikely of ways and, in some cases, entirely made up. This one is of Rome. I study a few photos until I find what I'm looking for: Gary reminded me of it, and I somehow held onto it all the way home. It's the Jesuit church of St Ignazio. I remember a wonderful mural inside, painted all up the walls and ceilings. I thought of it when Gary talked about seeing a 3D picture on a 2D screen, because the paintings on the walls combine to produce the most extraordinary optical illusion of having *depth* to them; stacked levels of heaven. And the damned thing is, I'll never know whether I genuinely remembered it from long ago - the pre-dementia Art - or whether I saw it on Aisha's computer only recently; or even on the TV, the internet … who knows? I think, in the end, who cares? Memory is but the wayward child of wilful time and capricious imagination; captivating but inconstant, and not to be depended upon. I can't tell Aisha about it in any case, because Gary is right: she'll never believe me. But I find something in the other slides, and now I just have to wait for my opportunity to arise.

'I was thinking of going on holiday,' Aisha says, when we are eating dinner a couple of weeks later, 'Maybe Paris again, or Prague. I loved Prague.'

It was a safe bet that she'd suggest a holiday sooner or later - I know both Maria and her sister have been urging her to take a break for ages.

'Not Rome,' I say, casually. 'It's too hot this time of year.'

'True,' she agrees, 'although we never did get to see the Vatican.'

'Well, in that heat, I don't think either of us wanted to queue that long.'

'No,' she says uncertainly, giving me a wondering look.

'Still, that castle was an interesting choice instead,' I remark, cheerfully forking up some more pasta. 'And what a view from the top!'

'You mean the Castel St Angelo?' she asks, staring at me,

but I'm not falling for that.

'Can't remember what it's called,' I say apologetically. God, this is easy; it's *easy*! Of course it was hot. Rome is always hot at that time of the year. There are always queues for the Vatican, it stands to reason: it's the Vatican. The Castel St Angelo is just across the river from St Peter's Square, and it was bound to have a good view from the top.

'Yes, that's the name. Never mind,' she says, with a bright smile.

I feel a twinge of guilt but, after all, it's in a good cause. Now, if I can only wriggle out of the inquisition that comes next, because I can't remember *everything*. I'm not being much more sophisticated than last time, to be honest, but at least I've not made the mistake of trying to put in too much detail. But fortune is on my side this time, and I know it, because Aisha doesn't want to be disappointed again.

'Do you still have your beach memory?' she asks me instead, throwing me slightly.

'Yes,' I say cautiously, 'but I think now it wasn't a beach at all. It was just a stretch of sandy path; that must have been where I was confused. I don't remember where it was. Anyway, it was when Maria was little; she was picking up snail shells. Those little stripy ones.'

I made that up completely, I'll admit, but it's exactly the sort of thing she would have done, I know *that*, somehow, even if it's only from all those early shows of Maria digging up worms, Maria in rock pools catching crabs, Maria peering at tadpoles; and if Aisha rings up later to ask her, she'll just laugh and say, "Oh, probably Mum. I don't really remember, to be honest."

'That's sweet,' Aisha says, with a genuine smile.

Another guilty twitch, but to be honest it doesn't last because, in the end, it's just not that important. It's not the event that matters, it's the emotion. The association.

I don't remember the birth of our daughter, not a minute.

I don't remember her first day at school, or her first love, or her graduation, or most of her life. All I have are small, insignificant fragments that don't fit together. I don't remember the first time I met my wife. I don't remember our wedding, or the first time we made love. But I remember a life, and a mind shaped by Maria and Aisha, and a hunger for the impression they made in those little wires in my brain, to fill gaps I cannot perceive; not with what has gone, but what will *be*, because some part of me knows that it will still fit. And some other part of me knows, it's all an illusion, but it's *my* illusion, and I'll believe it if I want to.

'Love,' I say, a little while later, 'why don't we go somewhere new for a holiday? Somewhere we haven't been before.'

'What a great idea.' And we fall to making plans. I may even remember to take pictures but, probably, in the moment, I'll forget. I usually do.

FANTASY

SPIRIT OF THE FOREST

By Pauline E. Dungate

The sound of claws on wood told Hunter that there was a Bengal tiger on the deck above. It didn't surprise him, despite his boat being moored on a tidal waterway in Sussex. A short while later, the door to his main cabin opened and Phoebe Makhani came down the steps. She was a tall woman. Her dark hair, curling about her shoulders, had a degree of muzziness that was almost deliberate. Her leathers, red flashed with black, emphasised her figure.

'Have you a current pilot's licence?' she asked.

'Yes. Why?'

'You will need it.'

'Why?'

'We are going to Ecuador.' Her tone was imperious as might be expected from a creature at the top of the food chain, except he knew that she did not eat meat. That hampered her activities and was the reason why she sometimes employed Hunter to assist her. Her dietary choice meant that she was strictly a creature of the night and needed him as her day-time eyes.

'I suppose, your presence here wouldn't be connected to the job offer I've received,' he said. Hunter made his living tracking animals. This might be a safari expedition for a wealthy client who wanted to see a particular animal in the wild, such as a snow leopard. On occasion, he tracked and captured creatures that had to be removed from an area for their own safety, perhaps because of a commercial project. Then they were either released elsewhere or homed in zoos as conservation breeding stock until a suitable habitat became available. Rarely, he tracked beasts that had become a danger to people or livestock. Over the last few days, he had been in correspondence with Andrees Suarez concerning the possible removal of an anaconda.

'We may have a common goal,' she said. 'Tell your friend to meet you in Coca.'

'When?'

'Three days from now.'

'Then what?'

'We resolve the issue of the big snake.'

'You think it's one of your kind?'

'That is what I intend to find out.' Phoebe was a shape-shifter. She could, at will, transform into a tiger. During his first encounter with her, Hunter had learnt that most of her kind kept to themselves but the pressures of human expansion exposed their sanctuaries. Most were carnivores and when they stepped over the boundary to acquire a taste for human flesh, she intervened.

Hunter brushed his fingers through his short, blond hair. 'I will have to book flights and arrange an import licence for my gun.'

'No need. The plane is at the airfield. Just collect what you will need and we can be on our way.'

'Just like that?'

'Exactly.'

Shoreham airfield was a ten-minute walk away from the River Adur and Hunter's mooring. It was a hub for private flying clubs and those who wanted an easy hop across the channel. The two-seater jet stood on the tarmac in front of one of the hangars. It was painted in red and black, the same patterns as on the motorbike that Phoebe usually rode, and the flashes on her leathers.

'Think you can fly that?' she asked.

It was faster than the machines he had trained on but the basics were bound to be the same. 'I might need a bit of tuition,' he said.

'I will give you that as we go. I have already filed a flight plan. We will refuel on the Azores, and at Rio. You will do the daytime flying.'

Hunter stowed his gear in the surprisingly large cargo space. This, he realised, was where Phoebe's Suzuki went when she was crossing continents. He climbed into the co-pilot's seat and fastened his harness. Phoebe was already settled at the controls and speaking to the control tower. This was a busy little airfield with a fair number of flights in and out during darkness, especially in the summer. It was also the base for a Coastguard helicopter.

Knowing he was likely to have sole control of the jet later, he watched Phoebe closely as she taxied to the head of the runway for take-off.

Theirs was the last flight into Coca, a commercial town on the Napo River. They landed in the dark, in driving rain. After parking in their allotted space, Hunter and Phoebe ran for the shelter of an open hangar. A steward gave them a ride to the main arrivals hall where Andrees was waiting for them. He was an Ecuadorian of European descent sporting a neat black beard. Hunter had met him on previous visits to the country and appreciated his wide knowledge of indigenous fauna.

'Are you sure you wish to travel at night and in the rain?' Andrees asked by way of greeting.

Hunter introduced Phoebe, who said, 'Dark I have no problem with. I hope your boat has an awning. I do not wish to get wet unless it is absolutely necessary.'

Hunter knew she could swim - he had seen her - but like many cats, she preferred not to.

They followed Andrees out to his car. 'I'll be coming with

you,' he said. 'To make sure all the accommodations are satisfactory.'

'Have there been problems?' Hunter asked.

'Not so much in the lodges but some of the local people are wary about being away from home at night.'

'Because of the snake?'

'Yes. Some believe it is a spirit sent to punish them for forsaking the ways of the forest.'

Motorised canoe was a misnomer. The blue-painted boat might be the right shape but it had seats for thirty people and room to spare for luggage. The canopy was high enough for Hunter to walk under it easily.

Andrees handed them life-jackets with an apology. 'Regulations, I'm afraid.' He also gave them a rain cape each. 'There is likely to be a fair amount of spray. Do you speak Spanish, Ms Makhani?'

Phoebe nodded. 'It is a language I am familiar with.'

'Good. Many of the local people don't speak English.'

As they passed under the bridge, the lights of the town dwindled in the distance. The banks of the river were dark and their distance was difficult to judge. Towards the centre, in the deeper channels, were the lights of transports. They carried entire trucks and tankers.

Hunter settled next to Andrees, his back to the river, and leant close to be heard over the engine and the sound of the water scooping up against the hull. 'Tell me more about this snake that I have come to find,' he said.

'Anacondas usually remain in the forest. Small ones hunt hoatzin, bigger ones take larger mammals, or caimans. It is rare for them to enter the villages.'

'Will they attack jaguar?' Phoebe asked.

'A cub or a juvenile, maybe. It would not be a sure contest.'

'What about our quarry?' Hunter asked.

'It took only chickens at first, then a pig. It might not have been the same one. The attacks were several weeks apart.

The local people were sanguine. That is what happens when you live in the forest.'

'What changed?'

'It took a child.'

'Fuck.'

'Is that certain?' Phoebe asked.

'The mother saw it.'

'How long ago?' Hunter asked.

'Three weeks. I emailed you after the news filtered through to us. I would prefer it to be captured. It can be re-released well away from any village.'

'That might not be possible,' Phoebe said.

'How big is it?' Hunter asked.

'Big enough to swallow a pig. I wouldn't want to rely on the mother's account. She was understandably hysterical.'

'And a meal like that would last it how long – four to six weeks?'

'Yes. It may be hungry soon.'

Hunter sighed. 'Phoebe is right. Taking down a large mammal is relatively easy, cold-bloods are harder. It takes longer for the tranquiliser to work, and that might put others in danger.'

Andrees said, 'Much as I hate the idea of destroying such a magnificent creature, it will be your judgement. The country needs tourists. If there is a man-eater around, they'll not come. The publicity will be too bad.'

They lapsed into silence, Hunter watching the shore as if he could see through the darkness to where his quarry was hiding. It wasn't the tranquiliser problem that disturbed him, it was the fact that Phoebe was here. That put a very different complexion on the problem.

Half an hour later, the boatman cut the engines and the craft drifted up to a small wooden jetty. There were electric lights here and Hunter could hear the purr of a small generator. Two local men caught the ropes thrown to them and tied the craft up. Andrees stepped ashore first. He introduced them. 'Oscar and Benares will be taking us up to the lodge.'

The two men paddled the canoe along a narrow, shallow waterway. The rain had stopped. Hunter felt that all the mosquitoes in the area were making up for lost time on his body. Phoebe seemed unperturbed. In the light of the lamp mounted on the prow, he could see the moths, midges and the occasional bat swooping after them.

After an hour, the creek widened and they emerged onto a lake alive with the eye-shine of caimans. Across the other side, the lights showed a cluster of terracotta-coloured buildings. As they glided into the moorings, Andrees said, 'Benares will show you to your lodge, then just follow the path up to the dining room. There'll be a meal waiting for us.'

Phoebe said, 'I hope you will excuse me. All I will need is some fruit. Perhaps you can bring it to my room, Hunter. After you have eaten.'

Considering that everything had to be brought in along the route they had taken, the food was very good. It was served by Donna de la Maza, the assistant manager of the site. She smiled a welcome as Andrees introduced her. She was a short, stocky woman.

'Thank you for waiting up for us,' Andrees addressed her in Spanish.

She replied in English. 'It is no problem.'

'I hope Andrees explained that I don't know how long myself and Ms Makhani will be staying.'

'He explained that you were naturalists interested in animal behaviour. Is that correct?'

'More or less. Our main interests are nocturnal, so we may well be out after dark.'

'Be careful, señor. Dangerous animals roam the forests

at night.'

'I shall watch for them.'

Seemingly satisfied, she disappeared into her domain at the rear of the building. Andrees spooned up the last of his ice-cream and said, 'I thought you always worked alone.'

'I do,' Hunter told him.

'Who is she?' Andrees gestured in the general direction of the downslope lodges.

'Phoebe Makhani is my… sponsor. It was her aircraft we flew in on. She was coming to this area, but she has her own agenda. I believe she is more interested in jaguars than reptiles.'

'She might have difficulty seeing any.'

Hunter shrugged. 'That's her problem. Tomorrow, I hope you can take me to the village. I'd like to see where the anaconda came out of the forest.'

'How do you intend to find it?'

'Modern technology and local knowledge. Do you suppose that either Oscar or Benares would act as guide?'

'I can ask them.'

Returning to the lodges later, Hunter hadn't expected Phoebe to be at home when he knocked on her door. He looked around him. If she was out there, she would be keeping to the shadows. He placed the fruit on her mat and retired.

Benares was waiting for them on the jetty the next morning. He was the younger, and slightly taller, of the two men that had brought them up the creek the night before, though he seemed very short beside Hunter's six-foot-two.

'Is Ms Makhani coming?' Andrees asked, arriving a few minutes later.

Hunter smiled. 'As you pointed out last night, I work alone.'

'Let's go then.'

Benares untied the canoe and paddled them across the lake in a slightly different direction from where they had originally come. Hunter took the opportunity to examine the site in daylight. The round painted buildings stood out against the green backdrop of forest, their thatched roofs blending with the vegetation. They were scattered up the side of a steep hill, a refuge against the flooding that was likely during the wet season. The hill was crowned by a robust wooden tower attached to one side of the dining room. It provided a good lookout across the lake. The other side, and the direction in which they were heading, appeared to be a solid barrier of plant growth. It was deceptive. The canoe glided into another creek that wound through the under-storey. Spider monkeys leapt, chattering, across the watercourse. A group of hoatzin huffed at them. With their spiky crests, Hunter thought they looked like punk versions of chickens.

The village itself consisted of about twenty houses carefully spaced throughout a clearing, giving each a patch of land to cultivate. Most had an area fenced off for animals, either goats or pigs. Hunter noticed that all the buildings were on stilts, even the central, community house. All homes were neatly constructed from local timber, each having television aerials and power lines leading to the central house, from where he could hear the hum of a generator. Benares pointed to it. 'That is our school and our hospital,' he said in Spanish.

Hunter replied in the same language. 'Would the woman who saw the snake be willing to talk to me?'

'She has lost her child.'

'I want to find the creature that stole it. I want to stop it stealing any other children.'

'I will ask,' Benares said. 'And I will find our head man.'

'What do you hope to do?' Andrees said.

'Most animals attack people because they find them easy

prey. It might be because they are hurt, or they have a taste for it.'

'Is that true of reptiles as well as mammals?'

'It will have a home area in which it hunts. If the village is in its area, it will hunt there.'

'Reptiles are normally shy.'

'Tell that to the couple who were attacked by caimans last year.' The crocodilians where supposed to hunt only at night making lakes in their territories safe for day-time bathing. The savaging of two Ecuadorian visitors had been played down so that tourists weren't scared away. Hunter didn't trust the piranha that infested these waters either.

Miguel, the headman, was smaller than Benares, his face creased into wrinkles. He wore jeans and a t-shirt advertising Coca-Cola. His baseball cap sported a Vodafone logo. He looked Hunter up and down, before folding his arms. 'Are you the one who will remove the spirit of the forest?' he asked.

'I have been asked to remove the anaconda from the area.'

'How will you do that, señor?'

'I don't wish to harm the creature but if that is the only way to protect your community, I will consider it.'

He unfolded his arms. 'I will show you where it has been seen, señor.'

'Gracias.'

Miguel took them to the end of the village where a small overgrown tributary joined the larger creek. A swampy area, clear of trees, crossed by a wooden walkway that disappearing into the forest on the far side.

'The boy was taken from here?' Hunter asked. It was good anaconda territory. The snake would be at home in the water and in the branches of the taller trees.

'From near the forest edge. He and his brother were fishing.'

Hunter walked along the wooden path, scanning the

vegetation on either side. Water gleamed between the plants and he caught flashes of silver where piranha lurked. Where the aerial roots of the mangroves touched the water, they provided ideal places to wait in ambush. A trio of hoatzin huffed at him before flapping awkwardly deeper into the understorey.

'Are there other places where the anaconda has been seen?' he asked Miguel.

'Benares will show you.'

Hunter spent the rest of the morning setting up infrared cameras around the village and other likely places the anaconda might go. He was unlikely to get immediate results but it would give him an idea of what animals used the trails. Where prey travelled, carnivores were likely to lie in wait.

Andrees showed him the tower that let to a platform in the canopy. It gave a fine view of the lake and the surrounding forest. He set up another camera there.

'It could be anywhere out there,' Andrees said.

'If it thinks there's easy food in the village, it will return there. That is where I'll be spending a lot of my time.'

'Have you ever failed to catch your quarry?'

'Yes. Most of the failures weren't man-eaters. I'm still looking for an albino python. Do you think you could find out who has moved to the area recently?'

'Certainly. How will this help with your quest?'

'It may not.' Hunter wasn't prepared to elaborate, though if Phoebe was right, a newcomer might explain why the anaconda had only been sighted in recent months.

At dusk, there was a tap on Hunter's door. He was refreshed after a shower washed off all the mud he had accumulated during the afternoon. As he opened it, Phoebe stepped inside.

She poured herself a glass of his water and sat on his bed, curling her feet up under her. 'Did you discover anything useful?' she asked.

'Only that there is an anaconda, and it is a big one. I've set up cameras along trails that it might use. This could be a long job.'

'I have met with Jaguar. He wishes Anaconda moved on. Being here, it is difficult for his tribe. They rely on tourists for their wealth.'

Hunter didn't question her statement. He was getting used to the idea that some animals were not what they seemed, and if the local shape-shifter was willing to help, he wouldn't say no.

'How will your machines help you?' she asked.

'I would prefer to spend part of the night monitoring them. It would be easier from the village if I could get across there.'

'It can be arranged.'

'Good. Will you eat with us tonight?' he asked.

She nodded. 'I shall make an arrangement with Jaguar to cross to the village first.'

When Hunter made his way up to the restaurant, Andrees was waiting for him. As Donna served them, he said, 'Now you are settled, I'll be heading back to Coca in the morning.'

'Thank you for all your help,' Phoebe said, joining them at the table and helping herself from a bowl of rice and vegetables.

'Would you like chicken or pork?' Donna asked her, placing the drinks Andrees and Hunter had ordered down on the table.

'Neither, thank you. I am a vegetarian.'

'Have you been working here long, Donna?' Hunter asked.

'About six months, señor. Why do you ask?'

'I'd heard that there is a high turnover of personnel, because of the isolation.'

'That is so. I am not yet bored. I like the forest around here and I can shop on-line. The satellite signal is good.'

'Didn't the teacher in the village arrive about the same time?' Andrees asked.

'We arrived on the same boat.'

'Does she sleep in the village?'

'She has accommodation here and goes across daily. Children from several villages attend her lessons.'

Donna moved off to speak with the other guests who had just arrived in the dining room.

Oscar was the boatman who met Phoebe and Hunter at the jetty. Already, caimans were gathering. River bats swooped close to the lights, chasing after moths. The sounds from the forest could have been any kind of creature. It was easy to imagine the country alive with spirits.

Miguel met them at the landing stage. 'It will be safer if you monitor the cameras from the community house.'

As Hunter followed him, he glanced back in time to see Phoebe morph into her tiger form and fade into the underbrush. He paused a moment, wondering that she had done that in front of Oscar. There was no sign of the boatman but a jaguar, sitting on the landing stage, stared at him for a moment before following Phoebe into the darkness.

Hunter set up his laptop, checking to see that all the cameras were working correctly. Each was triggered by movement in the field of view and he could easily download images from them. Donna had been right – the signal was good.

'Do not be surprised, señor,' Miguel said. 'Our lives might be simple but we are not primitive. Most of the men here are Rangers, guiding visitors through the forest. Many of them also have homes in Coca and wish to keep in touch with their families.'

'I thought the families were here.'

'Wives and children, yes. Grandparents and cousins often prefer comfort. Will you show me what your cameras see?'

Hunter wasn't sure he could refuse. He just hoped that the tiger didn't walk along a trail while Miguel was watching. That would be difficult to explain. The impression he got from Phoebe was that her kind kept their natures secret from regular humans and only rarely, such as in his case, did they expose themselves. He needn't have worried. Miguel's attention was soon drawn away by another villager wanting his advice.

Only three cameras had picked up anything: a party of giant otters cavorting in the creek, a tapir wandering up a track and a rat-snake crossing the canopy platform.

Phoebe joined him, in human form, around midnight. 'Jaguar believes that Anaconda will not be abroad before full moon.'

'That is in ten days. Does Jaguar have a reason for this belief?'

'He has been counting the nights between the attacks.'

'But doesn't know where Anaconda is hiding?'

'No. He is sure she is one of our kind.'

'She?'

'Jaguar is sure that Anaconda is female.'

'If Anaconda is eating meat, she could be awake during daytime. She could have a job in the area.'

'That is so.'

Hunter frowned. When he had first met Phoebe, she had explained that, although she could change into one, she chose not to feed the tiger. That limited her to night-time activity as long as her human form remained vegetarian. Once, it had not been a problem that the shifters ate meat as the human population was much sparser but, as the wilderness areas shrank encounters between the two races was inevitable. Carnivores are lazy. They catch what is easiest. Humans are easy prey. While the human form could fit into society, the animal form would take what it wanted, when it wanted. Most shifters kept away from the cities. Only a rogue would be prepared to accept the danger of living amongst the luxury modern technology offered. As Phoebe had explained, as long as they stuck to feeding their animal on the local fauna, they were safe. The danger was when the craving for meat crossed the line. Anaconda had done that by taking the child.

'How long do you intend to stay?' Phoebe asked.

'Not much longer. I can pick up the data tomorrow, and I do need to sleep at night.'

'Oscar will take you back when you are ready.'

'What about you?'

'There are other ways of reaching my lodge than by crossing the water.'

The next ten days followed the same pattern. Only once did Hunter catch a glimpse of an anaconda on one of his cameras. Both he and Phoebe thought it too small to be the one they were after. A conversation with Dolores, the teacher, didn't give him any clues that she was other than she seemed. Neither did his observation of a few of her lessons. She was here, she said, because she believed all children should have an education without having to board away from their families.

Hunter spent the days looking for possible places the snake would hunt based on the other animals that used the trails. He never went unarmed. The rifle slung over his shoulder was loaded with tranquilisers, useful against human and beast. Though he had a knife in a sheath at his belt, he carried a machete. In forest conditions, it helped clear a passage. He changed the position of some of his cameras and set a couple further away.

The night before the full moon, Phoebe sat on his bed again. 'Jaguar suggests using bait.'

'I can ask Miguel if he can spare a pig. Tell me, how did you know where Michael Tan was?' Tan was the shifter that Phoebe had been hunting when they had first met. Hunter was tracking him in his animal form at the same time.

'I had been following him for a long time.'

'So you can't tell if either Donna or Dolores are Anaconda.'

'No. I have to see them change.'

'But you knew Oscar.'

'Jaguar had already asked me for help, just as Andrees had asked you.'

'Is it one of them, or could there be another candidate?'

'I do not know. Bait is still a good idea. Where will you tether it?'

'On the boardwalk, where the child was snatched. That may be where the anaconda comes out of the forest.'

'But, as she walks in daylight, you will need to have it in place soon after noon. I doubt Anaconda will feed before then.'

Miguel was willing to volunteer one of his own pigs. The animal wasn't as happy. Used to having the freedom of the village, it squealed its protest at being tethered, unable to flee from the edge of the forest. The water didn't bother it as, twice in the first half hour, it leapt from the boardwalk into the swamp. Discovering that it couldn't swim away, it clambered back onto the dryer surface. Hunter had fitted an electronic tag to the pig. If it was dragged away, they would at least know where it had been taken to, and it was unlikely to shed it.

An opportunity to talk to Dolores arrived when school broke for lunch. Hunter was sitting on the steps of the community hut when the children escaped with whoops of delight and headed straight for the water's edge.

When she appeared in the doorway, he said, 'Don't they worry about being attacked by caimans or piranha?'

She considered his question. 'Piranha are not dangerous unless you are cut. Caimans only hunt at night.'

He knew the perceived wisdom but wasn't prepared to put it to the test. 'What about the anaconda?'

'The one you are trying to catch? While the children stay together, they are safe. It will only pick off lone prey. Like your pig.'

Hunter had been unsure about whether he should tell Dolores about that or not. If she was Anaconda, she would avoid the bait. Phoebe had told him that the shifter would take pleasure in thwarting his plan. 'Why don't you join me for lunch?' he asked.

'Why not? Just let me get mine.' She disappeared back into the hut and returned with a plastic box similar to the one Hunter had been given his lunch in. Inside, there was a wrap of rice and beans with fruit and a slice of cake.

After they had eaten, she said, 'Could I see what you have found on your cameras?'

'Certainly.' He rinsed his fingers with a spill from his water bottle before opening his laptop. 'I had hoped to catch the anaconda on camera, but no luck. I was very pleased to see a jaguar on this trail.'

She leaned forward to examine the grainy pictures but made no comment.

After they went their separate ways, he spent the rest of the afternoon changing the positions of the cameras she had seen images from.

Hunter had ordered an early supper, intending to spend most of the night in the village. He was disappointed when Donna didn't serve him, though right at the end of the meal, she did appear to ask if he wanted coffee.

'May I have a flask?' he said. 'I shall be out most of the night.'

It was not fully dark when Hunter returned to the village. An agitated Miguel met him. 'The pig. It is gone.'

'Shit. Did the snake take it?'

'No-one saw.'

The arrangement had been for someone to keep watch but he could understand mothers wanting their children – even the older ones – indoors once night had fallen. Hunter sat down on the jetty and opened his laptop, selecting the camera for the bait's position, and downloaded.

On the screen, he saw a woman walk along the boardwalk, then bend down and untie the pig. It wandered off into the forest. The woman followed it. Just as she reached the edge of the camera's range, there was a blurring of the image. He played it through several times. If he used his imagination, it could seem that she morphed into a snake. She had had her back to him the whole time but he doubted Donna could have reached there before him. He couldn't be sure that it was Dolores either.

'That was Anaconda,' Phoebe said from beside him. He'd been so intent on the screen that he hadn't noticed her arrival. 'Was the pig tagged?'

'Yes.'

'Then I will hunt, and you will use your electronics.'

How far they would have to go would depend on the head-start the pig had. Oscar, who had stayed beside the boat said, 'I will take you across the water, if you need to go.'

Hunter set the frequency for the pig's tag, and frowned. Constricting snakes like anacondas were mainly ambush hunters so why would Dolores, if it was her, release the pig and trail it into the forest? It was aberrant behaviour. If they could find her, capturing her should be easy. Constrictors needed time to swallow a meal then were soporific while they digested it, so it wasn't likely to go far.

Hunter scanned the area. The bleep from the tag appeared

to be coming from the southern side of the lake. Following the signal, he had Oscar paddle him across. He fitted his night vision goggles in place. Phoebe and Oscar wouldn't have problems in the dark but Hunter was human, and night-blind.

Once on dry land, Oscar morphed into Jaguar and padded at Hunter's heels. It made him feel uncomfortable, despite knowing that the shifter wouldn't hurt him. He recognised some of the trees they passed. This was the track that led to the canopy tower. As they approached, Hunter thought he had lost the signal. When he found it again, it was above him.

He stood at the foot of the tower and looked up wondering if the pig had voluntarily climbed the steps, or if it had been dragged. The forest around him was quiet; the kind of hush that descends when a predator is around. One, a jaguar, sat three feet away watching him. He didn't know where Phoebe was. Hunter unslung his rifle and checked that the tranquiliser rounds were in position. Then he started to climb.

He went cautiously, pausing every few steps to listen. A breeze amongst the leaves could easily be misinterpreted as the slither of scales on wood. In the dark, it seemed a long way up.

Hunter emerged onto the platform which had a high rail around it and surrounded the bole of one of the highest trees in the area. Thick branches spread out above him. The trunk obscured much of the surface, including where the pig must be. Since there was no noise other than the steady beep of his instrument, he had to assume it was dead and that its killer was close by. He scanned the upper branches before slowly moving away from the stairs, keeping close to the railing to give himself the widest view.

A hoof came into sight first, unmoving. He edged around and more of the pig came into view. Then he saw the anaconda. Most of its body lay on the platform. Its mouth widening as it dislocated its jaw to begin swallowing its prey. It stopped as it spotted Hunter's movement and slowly closed its mouth. He raised his rifle. He needed a good shot behind the head, clear of the skull.

Pain erupted in his shoulder. A thousand needles penetrated his skin. His shot went wild as coils wrapped around his chest, squeezing.

Fuck, he thought, *there are two of them.*

Fur brushed his leg. There was a moment of stillness. Blackness edged his vision. He couldn't breathe.

'Release him, or she dies.' Phoebe stood over the first anaconda. One hand was hooked in the creature's mouth, preventing it closing, the other was placed just behind the head. The pressure on his chest eased slightly. He took a deep, shuddering breath. 'I mean it,' Phoebe said.

Hunter saw the shimmer as she became Tiger just long enough for him to see the extended claws poised to puncture the spinal chord. He felt the coils around him retract, then Donna was standing on the platform beside her.

'Don't kill her,' she said.

'Give me a reason not to,' Phoebe said. 'You know the rules. Or did your parents neglect your education?'

'She is my sister,' Donna said.

'She has broken the rules. The penalty is death. You know that.'

'It is the nature of carnivores to hunt.'

'I still have no reason not to execute her, here, now.'

'It is not fair to confine us to a twilight world, to be unable to live our human lives.'

'She killed a human child. Even amongst their kind, that is a reason for death.'

'This is not your country.'

Phoebe glanced at Hunter. 'This man thinks there is another way.'

He nodded. 'My choice would be to confine her to a zoo and live the rest of her life as a captive.'

'No!' Donna took a step past him.

He saw the shimmer as she began to change. He looped an arm around the woman's neck and hugged the anaconda's head to his chest. His other hand drew the knife from his belt and held it at her throat. 'There is a third way,' he said.

Donna changed back. 'What way?'

'This is still a country of wilderness. I will take both of you to the deepest part, away from human habitation. I will free you under certain conditions.'

'What are they?'

'That you swear to stay away from human habitation, you agree to be tagged so we will know if you break your word.' Hunter knew that Dolores would never be convicted in a human court but Phoebe would execute without qualms. Hunter disliked the idea of killing any wild creature, unless necessary.

'If we agree, you will free us?' She sounded sceptical.

'If Jaguar accepts the compromise,' Phoebe said. 'It is his country.'

'I do.' Oscar padded from the top of the staircase, morphing to human as he did so. 'The tags will mean that other Jaguars will know that you keep your word. Do you accept?'

Donna nodded. Phoebe stepped back to allow Dolores to take human form.

It was Andrees that arranged a helicopter to carry the two tagged anacondas to a distant, unmapped part of the Amazon basin as part of the conservation programme. Hunter packed and said his farewells, and joined Phoebe and Oscar for the night ride back to the main Napo River. As he waited to board the motorised canoe for the return trip to Coca, he heard Oscar say, 'Tiger, you have chosen your human well.'

Hunter grinned as he heard her reply. 'He has his uses.'

MISTRESS OF FORTUNE

By Kim Gravell

'Hey, Tarot!'

Cal glanced back along the forest road towards the caravan, and the lanky form sitting patiently holding the Duchess' reins. The mare was making the most of the unscheduled stop. With one hind hoof cocked and her head drooping, she looked the picture of relaxation. Even the measured swish of her tail, keeping the autumn flies at bay, was peaceful. Sitting alongside Tarot, on the driver's bench, Rose swung her bare feet idly. It was difficult to tell what, if anything, was going through that pretty head.

'Get your scrawny carcass down here and have a look at this.'

Without waiting for a reply, Cal turned his attention back to the fallen trunk blocking their path. Around him, the forest was still, the earth exhaling dampness and the green scent of crushed plants. Tarot handed the reins to Rose and swung soundlessly to the ground. No unnecessary questions, no pointless comments, just a spare, economy of movement; that was Tarot. For no discernible reason, Cal was suddenly very glad that he'd agreed to let her travel with them. There was a comfort in having her there, like knowing you had a hidden blade in your boot-top.

She had been there when he had finished the last story, the afternoon shadows already stretching and growing long across the hard-packed earth of Combe Hallows' fairground; a figure in grey sitting a little to one side of the small audience. He had only gone over to her to retrieve the stray leather ball lying at her feet, a remnant of Ilya's drunken juggler act. Yet, as he bent to grasp it, the woman's fingers closed around the ball and she stood up. Cal's eyes flicked to the ground and back. To some, it might have been mistaken for a gesture of shyness but, in reality, he was appraising his new companion. The clothes he had taken for grey were actually black, smudged liberally with the chalky white of road dust. Black trousers tucked into calf-high boots, a small amount of white shirt showing beneath a black jerkin and black drover's coat. The only thing colourful on her was a bandana of teal silk tied at her throat, glistening like the flash of colour on a mallard's wing. Even her eyes were monochrome; the flat grey of a winter sky.

Cal looked directly into those eyes and smiled his most open, friendly smile; the one he used when he was completely on guard.

'I hope you enjoyed our show, mistress, but we're finished for the day. There's no need to reserve a seat for later.'

Most people would have warmed to either the smile or the joke, but not this woman. She simply looked at him and there was neither hostility nor warmth in that look; in fact, there was nothing he could gauge from it at all.

The lack of reaction unnerved Cal, unreasonably so, given that she had done nothing to threaten him; but he felt he was being scrutinised, judged, and that was not something he took well. 'Nor do we encourage people to take a keepsake to remember us by.' His tone was sharper than he intended as he glanced at the ball in her hand, and the realisation of that fractional loss of control needled him further.

The woman continued to look at him, still showing no reaction to his words or the tone of his voice. Did she even understand what he was saying? Was she perhaps foreign? Or simple minded? But he sensed nothing of Rose's empty-headed simplicity behind that cold gaze.

'I do not seek a souvenir.' She tossed the ball to him and Cal plucked it automatically from mid-air, even as his mind stalled on the fact that she had finally spoken. 'I want to travel with you.'

While informal alliances of travellers, sharing the road for safety, were not uncommon, to the best of Cal's knowledge this woman had no reason to know their next destination. Internal alarms ringing, his response was blunt. 'We don't do protection.'

Was that a smile that twisted the corner of her mouth? Cal couldn't be sure; it was gone almost before it had a chance to register, but it was the first trace of emotion, the first trace of any human response, he had seen on her face.

'I am not in need of protection.'

Not for a second did Cal doubt her.

'You are travelling to Saint Martin's, as am I.'

How did she know that? It wasn't an unreasonable guess that they might be heading that way, seeking employment during the harvest, but the woman had phrased it as a fact.

'I believe I can be useful to you in that time, but I am also willing to pay for the privilege of your troupe's company.'

When he said nothing, she cocked her head on one side, looking very much like a crow, eyeing up the camp scraps and judging whether it could get to them and get away without being caught.

'What do you have to lose? You have my money and an additional pair of hands on the road. All I ask is that you give me the five days between here and there. If I've not proved my worth by then, I'll leave you.'

Cal said nothing, turning her proposition over in his mind. It wasn't as if what she asked was unreasonable. Nor was the troupe so well off that they could lightly turn down an opportunity to make money. He ran his eyes up and down her, openly this time, appraising her rather as if she were a horse he'd been offered for sale. It was deliberately rude, and a small part of him baulked at doing it, for he wasn't by nature a rude man; but she made no comment. If anything, he had the impression she knew what he was doing and was amused by it.

He made his decision, but he couldn't let it go at that; he wanted to know more about her. 'What can you do?'

'I read the Cards.' For a moment there was challenge in those cold-fish eyes. 'I do not earn my keep on my back.'

The troupe master weathered the gaze, considering her words and the wealth of things she had not said, but that her words implied. She was almost as tall as he was. Not pretty; striking perhaps, if you liked cheekbones that would cut air and a body that was thin as whip cord. Tumbling her would be like rutting with a picket fence. He nodded.

'Tomorrow morning, an hour after sunrise. If you're not here we'll go without you.'

She bowed slightly, a gesture reminiscent of Ilya accepting the audience's pennies. When she straightened, there were two silver pieces in her palm and even Cal, raised on sleight of hand, could only guess at where she had hidden them until that point.

It was only when she had gone he realised he had not asked her name.

She became known as Tarot. Each night, when the fire was banked and the camp was settling towards sleep, she would take her cards and lay them out one by one in some unfathomable pattern. She made no attempt to hide what she did, yet she shared nothing of what the turning of the cards revealed to her. Nor would she read the cards for any of them, although Cal knew Ilya had asked her. She had simply looked at the young juggler, an unreadable expression in those wintery eyes.

'When we get to Saint Martin's,' she said, and refused to be drawn as to why that might be.

That last night, Cal approached her as she finished laying out the cards. A storm had been rising steadily since the afternoon and the wind was already whipping the tree tops. Cal prowled the camp site, checking and re-checking that all their gear was stowed tight. He hated storms with a vengeance, knowing how vulnerable they were while on the road, and the tension of waiting for one to break sawed at his nerves. As leader, he counted himself personally responsible for the troupe's safety, and anything that took that out of his hands made him irritable and short tempered. He'd already reduced Rose to tears with one outburst and had been secretly relieved when Kat had taken the young woman inside the caravan. A change in the wind brought him a snatch of notes and the combination of two female voices rising in harmony through the bawdy chorus of a drinking song.

Stand up boys, let's be having you.
Stand up boys, we'll have some fun.

He listened as Kat's husky contralto picked up the words of the verse. She had changed them from the version he knew. This time it was the women who were having the fun and the soldiers they were addressing definitely weren't their husbands or partners. It wasn't that sort of fun. Rose might already have forgotten her fright but his sister was altogether less forgiving. Cal knew he would have to apologise later; knowing that he had been in the wrong did nothing to improve his mood.

Turning away from the caravan, he saw Tarot watching him. Sat cross legged on her bedroll, her cards laid out in front of her, she made no effort to hide it. She met his stare for a moment, saying nothing, her own face expressionless, then turned her attention once more to the patterns spread before her.

'Well?' he demanded.

When he got no response, he strode across and stood over her, staring down at the black scarecrow figure. His boot tips were almost trampling the spread cards but he refused to step away. Adrenalin surged in his blood, and he had a sudden urge to grab those thin shoulders and shake her to see if anything could rattle her supreme self-composure. When the first crack of thunder made him jump, he balled his hands into fists, furious that he'd allowed the storm's power to string his nerves like a mandolin. Lightning flashed on the horizon, bright as magnesium, outlining the camp in white and violet. No rain fell but, above the trees, the sky was grey and sulphurous. It would not be long in coming.

Of course, he reminded himself, Tarot had never actually said there was danger ahead. She had simply implied that something would happen on the road to Saint Martin's; something that she could help them deal with.

I believe I can be useful to you.

She could have been talking about anything. Or nothing. It was hard to imagine what could happen to them on the road that the presence of one scrawny woman would divert. Yet something deep within him had believed her, and believed her still, though he would have denied it to his last breath.

'Well?' he asked again, quieter now, and this time, somewhat to his surprise, she answered him.

'Tomorrow.'

With her thin, pale face and black clothes, she could almost have been a wraith, risen from a lonely grave. Cal shivered as a sense of otherworldliness swept over him. For a moment, the veil of reality seemed to thin and he wondered, not for the first time, who this woman really was.

Then Tarot spoke again, breaking the spell. 'It comes.' At that, she gathered the cards back into her pack and turned away from him, rolling herself in her blanket and settling down to sleep without another word.

So here he was, staring at the tree blocking their path. Its top was caught in a tangle of gorse and hawthorn on the far side of the road, just sufficient to keep it off the ground, so that it rose at an angle to almost hip height. Even a riding horse would have baulked at jumping it. Of course, even if it had been flat on the road, they wouldn't have been able to get the caravan over it.

Tarot scrutinised the earthy mass of the pine's root ball that had pulled free of the soil when it fell.

Cal had already examined it and knew what she would find. 'There's no sign of any digging to suggest it was brought down deliberately.'

Tarot nodded once, agreeing with his observations, if not necessarily with his conclusion.

'There are easier ways to block a road,' he added.

'But not without raising suspicions.'

'Well, it hardly matters. We can't go over it and we can't go round it.' He looked pointedly at the trees and scrub that were choking the ground to either side of the road. It would take hours of back-breaking effort to clear a path. Even then, they would risk cracking a wheel on the uneven ground. 'Bandits or not, we'll be here next Saturday if we don't shift this.' He brushed absently at the soil on the knees of his trousers. 'Ilya! We'll need the axe.'

Ilya and Kat had already materialised from the back of the caravan. Most of the morning, they had been practicing a new act, which involved Ilya freeing himself from an impressive array of bonds in time to save a swooning Kat from the clutches of the arch villain. Cal had yet to be convinced the piece wouldn't work better played for comic effect, with his sister rescuing a swooning Ilya. Certainly, it was more in keeping with their respective temperaments, although Ilya was the better contortionist. Still, they might work up both versions and surprise their audiences by switching between the two.

As Ilya disappeared to fetch the tools, Cal turned his attention back to the tree. If he cut the trunk midway, they could use the Duchess to haul the two halves off the road. He glanced up to see that Kat was already unfastening the mare's traces, and he flashed her a quick grin. Thirty seven years they'd faced the world together. Sometimes words simply weren't necessary to know what the other needed.

Tarot, on the other hand, was very much a mystery. Her hand on his arm was like a physical shock.

'This did not fall by accident.'

'No?' He felt the first stirrings of irritation at her secrecy and her *I know more than you do* pronouncements. For all he knew, she might have seen this in the cards but, if this was a trap, it had yet to show any sign of closing upon them.

'Well, no one's leapt out of the bushes to attack us now, have they? And if you have any suggestions as to how we get past, that don't involve an hour's work with an axe and a rope, I'll be glad to hear them. But we'll starve to death here before it shifts itself.'

She opened her mouth to retort and then stopped, turning her head as though to catch some distant sound.

'It begins,' she said and, despite himself, Cal felt a surge of adrenalin at the cold certainty in her voice. Then he heard the jingle of harnesses and the muffled clop of hooves moving towards them on the forest road.

He was about to yell to Ilya and Kat to get back to the caravan, when he caught sight of what it was that approached them and almost laughed aloud. If this was the danger that Tarot had foreseen, he certainly wasn't frightened. True, the older of the two was a big, bear-like man, whose tunic strained across his shoulders, but it also strained across a large belly, and the foppish tassels decorating his shirt and plum coloured boots spoke more of a merchant than a bandit. His younger companion was similarly broad, although he lacked his partner's belly or his round, rather generous face. He bore a pinched look that reminded Cal of nothing so much as a weasel, and a bad tempered one at that. He rode his slab-faced roan with his shoulders slumped, paying scant attention to his surroundings or to his companion. It was the older man who was first to realise that their way was blocked.

When he saw Cal staring at him over the body of the pine, he gave a theatrical squeak, dropped the reins and threw his hands up. 'Peace, friends.' His voice was surprisingly high pitched for such a big frame. 'We're only travellers. We mean you no harm.'

He nudged his friend and Weasel-face, who had started to reach for his belt knife, slowly raised his own hands to show good faith.

Cal turned to make a sarcastic remark to Tarot, but she was no longer at his side. Probably just as well. He turned back to the two riders with an apologetic shrug. 'Well met, gentlemen. As you can see, we have a small problem with our journey, but likely you can get past, if you don't mind leaving the road to do it.'

'Nonsense, my friend.'

The older merchant clambered down from his horse, which promptly put its nose down and started to lip at the cobbles, searching out the grass that grew at the edges of the road. 'It's a good job we happened along. Two more strong backs will soon make light of this, and we can all be on our way. My nephew and I will be happy to lend a hand, won't we Duncan?'

Duncan looked anything but happy, but he threw a leg over the roan's neck and dropped to the ground without comment. His face said all that was needed about both the tree and his uncle's offer.

'Do you have an axe? Ah, excellent.'

The merchant's voice had dropped slightly now he had got over his fright, and Cal was amused by the bustling efficiency with which he started to direct proceedings. On the ground, he was a couple of inches taller than Cal's own six feet; in his prime, he had probably been massively strong, but his face now showed the signs of too much good living, reflected in his ample girth. His thick fingers were bedecked with cabochon rings and Cal wondered if he could hold an axe, much less use one. Still, there was no denying his enthusiasm for organising things.

'Now, if you and I can cut through the trunk, I do believe my nephew and your young man …' he paused to beam at Ilya and the morose Duncan, ' … can get the top free. Go on then.'

He made small shooing motions with his hands and his nephew retreated sulkily to the far end of the trunk. Ilya hesitated for a moment, but went to join him at Cal's nod. The troupe leader could only hope his friend's easy going personality might rub off on the miserable Duncan. Had it not been for his uncle's unquenchable enthusiasm, Cal would have told the younger merchant to get back on his horse and clear off; he could do without help that came with a face like a wet Monday. But Uncle was adamant they should help, although Cal had made a bet with himself that he would still end up doing all the axe work.

'Then all we need do is to pull the two pieces aside, and the job will be done.' Another beaming smile and Uncle stretched his arms out theatrically wide. 'Let us begin,' he pronounced, clapping his hands together like a ringmaster summoning his first act.

'Bitch!'

The angry voice cut across the forest, almost as if Uncle's words had been a signal. Cal whirled towards the sound, just in time to see Rose leap back from the side of the road like a startled deer and streak towards the caravan. Behind her was a man with four bloody scratches running across his face, and an expression that promised no second chances when he caught her. He had a soldier's close-cropped hair, and his clothes, a mixture of dirty greens and browns, just right for fading unnoticed into woodland, were patched with iron and leather. Bandit, or mercenary leftover from the South Hold wars; neither was good news. Rose slipped a little as she scrambled up onto the driver's bench. The man snatched at her skirts, but a wooden bucket connected with the side of his head, sending him crashing heavily into the side of the van, the broken slats draped round his shoulders like a fancy collar.

The caravan door slammed shut behind Rose and, for a moment, it seemed the fight was over before it had properly begun. But the man Kat had crowned with the bucket was already getting to his feet, and Cal suddenly found he had problems of his own when the merchant, who had seemed to be as shocked as he was by this run of events, turned and swung at him.

While Cal had never been one to go seeking trouble, as a traveller he'd learned early to fight as hard and as dirty as was needed. So, while part of his mind was berating him for being so stupid as to fall for this ruse, the greater part of it was concentrating on getting him through the next few minutes without getting brained. It became clear very quickly that that wasn't going to be easy, Uncle's stiff and cumbersome gait of earlier proving to be no more real than his membership of the Merchants' Guild. Not only was he fast on his feet, but his greater height gave him several inches more reach than Cal.

He was fast with his hands too. Giving ground because he had to, Cal ducked back to avoid a swinging punch that would have knocked him into the middle of next week, only to have a left-handed jab nearly take him from the other side. Even as he jerked his head out of the way, he felt a sting as the edge of one of Uncle's rings laid his cheek open. He ignored it and threw in a short jab of his own, more as cover for a solid kick to the bandit's knee than any real hope he'd catch the man, though it never hurt to try. The kick wasn't as effective as he had hoped. Oh, it connected well enough, but his fancy boots were obviously lined with solid hide. That, or the man was wearing poleyn under his ridiculous damson suede. But, even though it didn't topple the bandit, it won Cal a second's grace in which to pull his belt knife.

Uncle backed off slightly at the sight of the blade, but his expression showed no concern. Against all expectation, he seemed delighted. A slow smile spread across his features, holding no hint of the genial merchant. This was a wolf's smile, feral, hinting at the pleasure of the hunt and the expectation of the kill.

'So you want to make a fight of it then, little tale-spinner?' Uncle laughed, turning with Cal as the troupe master circled warily round him. 'So much the better. I'm going to enjoy this.'

Still keeping his eye on Cal, he reached into the folds of one elaborately swaged sleeve, and pulled out a length of leather-wrapped wood, roughly as long as his forearm. He hefted it casually, so that the iron spiked ball at its end swung freely from its dozen links of chain.

A star mace. Damn!

Cal didn't wait to see how experienced Uncle was with the mace; he knew the likely answer already. Taking his life in his hands, he did the one thing he hoped the bandit wouldn't expect from him. Dropping his knife, he dived past the man, not for the clear space to his left, but to his right, almost into the branches of the pine, tucking his body into a forward roll. The edge of a granite cobble bit into his shoulder as he rolled, but he ignored it as his hands found damp earth and pine needles and a smooth oak shaft. He grasped the axe as his momentum took him past, pulling it flat against his body as he threw himself into a second roll.

He came out of the roll with his hands raised above his head, the axe solid in a double handed grip, the shaft angled down protecting head, neck and shoulder from attack. The move saved his life for Uncle had turned with him and was already swinging the mace in towards his head. It connected with the solid oak shaft, the vibration making Cal's hands throb. He ignored the sensation, sweeping the axe round in a fast arc, using the muscles of his arms and his sides to give it momentum, connecting solidly with the bandit's side before he could get the mace back for a second swing. It was the flat of the blade that hit but, even so, it was sufficient to knock the man sideways and Cal was already on his feet, following through to ram the head of the shaft up under the merchant's nose. Uncle went backwards into the pine branches, blood pouring down his face. He didn't get up.

Cal didn't bother to check on his opponent, his attention was already on Ilya and Duncan. It seemed the morose nephew did know how to smile, but only when he was fighting. Ilya went down under a roundhouse punch and, although the reflex of years of tumbling brought the young man back to his feet, it was clear he was in no condition to fight back. Perhaps Duncan realised he wasn't going to get much sport from his opponent, because suddenly there was a knife in his hand and he was advancing on Ilya with a deadly look in his eyes.

'Ilya! Down!'

Cal put the full force of his troupe master voice into the command, banking that Ilya would obey him unquestioningly. In one fluid movement, he bent and snatched up his belt knife from the cobbles, the blade spinning from his hand towards its target as the young juggler dropped to the ground in front of his opponent, as though pole-axed. Cal had a second's grace to see the almost-comical look of astonishment that blossomed on Duncan's face as the knife took him in the pit of the throat – had it never occurred to him that the troupe juggled with more than just balls? – then a huge shape lunged at him from the side and all he saw was the mace coming down at his head.

He just managed to get his left arm up so it was his forearm and not his head that took the blow. Cal felt bone splinter under the impact, even as the force of it sent him to his knees. Somehow, he managed to pull the hideout blade from his boot top, right handed and clumsy, as the shock scalded through him, turning muscles to water. He tried to counter, but a foot connected heavily with his wrist and the blade spun harmlessly from his grip.

It landed mere feet away, but it might as well have been on the other side of the moon for all the chance he had of reaching it. Not even the certain knowledge that he would die if he didn't move was sufficient to make his muscles obey him further. That he was still on his knees was little short of a miracle, but meant nothing save he would meet his death upright rather than face down on the ground. Time slowed as the studded iron ball reached its zenith and seemed to hang above him. Then it plunged towards his head, inexorable as summer lightning.

Looking back, Cal could never quite explain how the scabbard managed to get there first. He swayed back as the ball and chain wrapped itself round two and a half feet of black lacquer-work, a mere hand-span short of his head. As Uncle tried to jerk the ball free, a slender, black clad form interposed itself between him and Cal: Tarot.

The scene blurred and stretched, the weaving figures in front of Cal growing improbably tall, like characters from a storyteller's tale of how a forest demon, with red-gold hair, and an ice-eyed angel, took human form to fight over a traveller's soul. Behind them, the forest trees formed a multi-hued backdrop of green and early autumn golds. The air smelled of blood and sweat, and the resin-soaked sweetness of pine. Swaying with the effort of staying upright, Cal fought to retain his grip on consciousness, struggling to focus, to separate the whirl of limbs into blow and counter-blow.

Then, suddenly, it was over. The rush of movement stopped, the two figures freezing. Cal had no idea who had won, until he found himself face to face with Uncle as the man's knees buckled and he crumpled around the point of Tarot's blade. She pulled the weapon free as he folded, opening him up from sternum to hip, but Cal had seen from the man's eyes that he was already dead. He crashed face down beside the troupe master, like a broken-stringed marionette.

For a moment, time stood still. Cal stared down at the bandit's bulk, his own chest spasming, fighting for breath that would not come, as though it had been his flesh the blade had run through. A wave of blackness swamped his vision and, from a distance, he heard someone call his name, strange and mournful, like the cry of a gull far out at sea. A hand gripped his chin, flesh burning against the icy coldness of his skin, the fingers digging into his jaw, forcing his head up. Tarot's eyes seemed to flare silver as she locked him with her gaze. The world dissolved into those two silver orbs. How had he ever thought they were grey?

'Remain.'

He wasn't sure she spoke but the word reverberated in his mind.

'I'm not going anywhere,' he tried to say.

He thought she caught him as he pitched forward into darkness.

Cal opened his eyes and stared for a long while at the wall opposite his bed. It wasn't the first time he had woken here, but it was the first time he felt capable of staying awake for longer than it took to swallow a few mouthfuls of broth, or to be helped to the privy.

He guessed he was in the manor at St. Martin's, though he had only snippets of memory of what had happened since the troupe's encounter with the bandits. They surfaced unbidden, blurred with pain and the rising of fever. The last of them was particularly bad: Kat trying to coax him to swallow willow bark tea, which he had pushed away, asking for water instead, but vomiting it back almost as soon as he had swallowed it. He had seen fear in Kat's eyes, though she had kept it from her voice, telling him sweet lies that all would be well. And there, like a rock in the centre of the maelstrom, was Tarot. When it was clear he could keep nothing down, she had brought out a tiny flask of liquid, grey as ashes and half again as bitter when she forced it past his clenched teeth. Then there had been nothing but merciful oblivion, until he had awoken here.

Cal tried to tally up those awakenings, but his recollection was hazy and he could judge neither how long he had been awake, nor the periods of darkness in between. A tentative exploration of his jaw revealed unaccustomed bristles under his fingers. Surely he couldn't have been out of things for long enough to grow a beard? But it was more than mere stubble, and prickly as the God of Fools' hair-jockstrap. He scratched irritably and considered the strapped bulk of his left arm, lying on the coverlet. From what he could see of his fingers, poking out from a mass of bandages, the flesh was no longer swollen to drum tightness, but it was still puffy and mottled with the purple and yellow of fading bruises. It would be a while before that hand would hold anything usefully, let alone a razor.

He was contemplating his options when the door opened and Kat slipped inside. She seemed pleased, but unsurprised, to see him conscious.

'You're awake.' She smiled, setting down an armful of folded cloth on the linen press. 'Good. Tarot said you were likely to start taking some notice of the world this morning.'

'She did, did she?'

'Mmm. I thought it might be later, but she was right.'

Cal noticed there was a new warmth in Kat's voice when she spoke of the fortune teller. Previously, there had been a degree of reservation between them; two strong women fathoming each other out. It seemed they had come to some sort of understanding.

He knew it was irrational, that he owed Tarot his life, but he felt a sense of mounting irritation towards the lanky fortune teller. Their agreement had been that she could travel with them as far as Saint Martin's. Well, here they were, and yet she was still with them, poking her beaky nose where it didn't belong. She might almost be a member of the troupe, the way Kat was talking. That wasn't an idea that sat well with Cal.

Another thought occurred to him, cutting across his building indignation; one that was nowhere near as comfortable. 'Sweet Lady! The harvest! We're booked to spend three weeks in the fields and instead I'm here on my back.' He glared at his sister, as though it were her fault that he had only just woken up. 'And if that weren't bad enough, you're not working either because you're playing nursemaid. Kat, you know we need this money, so we don't have to travel over winter. We can't afford to be spending on lodgings and medicines and special treatment.'

'Don't you worry about the harvest.' Kat drew up a stool beside the bed. 'Tarot's been helping out, so we're only one pair of hands short, and I've been putting the time to good use. Needlework will sell, whatever time of year it's made.' She indicated the small pile of lavender bags on the nightstand, the top one embroidered with a posy of delicate flower heads. 'And now you're awake, there are plenty of jobs you can do while that arm's healing. I've a mind to send you to watch the youngsters when they go brambling.

Rose would do it, but she'd let them eat too many.' A trace of wickedness showed in her blue and green eyes. 'Although I could sell a lot of bellyache cures as a result.'

'This is still costing us money though,' Cal countered, not so easily mollified. 'Even if Tarot is helping out. Besides, what she earns is hers to keep; it's not as if she's part of the troupe.' He wanted to make that clear. No one joined without his say so. 'Although I appreciate her helping us keep our commitments to the manor,' he added grudgingly. 'But you shouldn't have to pay for this.'

Kat's lips thinned a little, and her voice was firm as she answered him. 'If I needed to spend my money, I'd spend it.' She raised a hand, cutting off his protest and then, surprisingly, she grinned, as smug as a cat on a sun-drenched windowsill. 'As it happens, I didn't need to.' The tilt of her chin told him he was going to have to ask to get the story out of her.

'Who paid then? Surely not Tarot?'

Please, no. He didn't want to be any more beholden to that walking scarecrow than he already was.

Kat smirked. 'Nope.'

'Kat...'

Kat could raise evasiveness to an art form when she wanted, but it seemed she was prepared to take pity on him just this once. 'We've come into some money while you've been asleep, dear brother. It turned out that our bandits had a price on their heads: a silver crown apiece for the four of them, plus we claimed bounty on their gear and the horses.'

'Four of them?' His recollection of what had passed since the fight was hazy but he was sure he remembered only three assailants.

'Four,' Kat confirmed. 'The two playing at merchants, that you and Tarot took care of, plus the one who made a grab for Rose. He made the mistake of following her into the van, by the way, and she split his head open with my best iron skillet.' She wrinkled her nose at the memory, and Cal's mind provided a graphic image of the result of Rose's action. 'There's one thing to be said for that girl: if you can get an idea into her head, it certainly sticks.'

'The Tale of the Drunken Miller.' Cal laughed softly. 'You always said it would work well in a fight.'

Rose's unlikely fighting prowess with cast iron cookware had started out as an attempt to get her to play the role of the irate mill-wife in the old morality tale. Unfortunately, the young woman had been unable to grasp the difference between pretending to hit someone with a saucepan and doing it for real. By the time they were forced to admit defeat, and abandon the scheme as too dangerous, she had already loosened Ilya's front teeth and managed to lay Cal out cold. It was Kat who had seen the act's potential as a defensive strategy.

'So that's the three I knew about.'

'Tarot took out one in the woods before the fighting started.' Kat paused for a moment, and then added thoughtfully, 'You know, she was very upset you were hurt. She blamed herself.'

'She shouldn't. She saved my life.' Even to his ears, he didn't sound very grateful.

'She did,' Kat agreed. 'And not just that once.'

Cal's mind conjured dark memories of Tarot and Kat talking together in the van, the corners lost to shadow and candlelight. He couldn't make out their words, but he knew what they were discussing. Nor did he need to see the look of desperation on Kat's face, whenever her glance slid towards where he lay, to know he was in serious trouble. He pushed the memory hastily away. 'I want to get up.'

Kat accepted the change of subject gracefully. 'I thought you might. That's why I've fetched you some clothes.'

Cal paused before crossing the courtyard. The stairs

had taken more effort than he had expected, and he was glad of the wall to lean his shoulder against. He pretended to be studying the condition of the lime plaster, while he caught his breath. He was equally glad that he'd refused Kat's offer to come with him. Already sick of being fussed over, he would have forced himself to stroll across the yard, all the way to the stables, if she'd been with him; even if it meant he risked fainting in the middle of the yard which, he grudgingly admitted to himself, would have been quite a strong possibility. As it was, there was no one to comment on the unshaven ruffian leaning in the shelter of the doorway, sucking in air like a broken-winded nag. The courtyard, and indeed the whole manor around it, was quiet, all but the smallest children being out with the harvesters.

The smallest children (*and invalids*, his inner voice added, maliciously). And those who looked after them. Tarot had chosen not to go with the harvesters that day, so Kat had said. It seemed the fortune teller thought he might want to talk to her when he woke up. Damned right he did. He snorted, pushing himself upright off the wall. *Bet she didn't need her cards for that prediction.*

He found Tarot, as Kat had suggested he might, in the stables. The large, barn-like building was quiet. Those of the manor's horses that weren't needed to pull the hay wains had been turned out to graze, but the faint sounds of someone working drew Cal in, through the beams of dusty sunlight and shadows, to a loose box at the far end of the row of empty stalls.

Without her black coat, the fortune teller looked thinner than ever; her white shirt sleeves were rolled back to expose bony wrists and forearms, and her teal-green bandana was tied around her forehead, to keep the sweat from her eyes as she worked. Watching Tarot sweep the body brush down over the mare's neck and shoulder, Cal could see the corded muscles in her forearm bunch as the Duchess leaned into the stroke, eyes half closed, her lower lip drooping with pleasure. Cal felt a surge of jealousy. It seemed that even the mare had turned traitor, finding in this stranger a suitable substitute for his attention.

As he stepped up to the stable door, Tarot lowered the brush and turned towards him, a fraction of a second before the mare opened her eyes and whickered, pushing past Tarot and extending her broad Roman nose for his caress.

'Get out of it, you old hay burner,' he muttered, somewhat mollified, as she lipped at his hair and then the sling across his chest. He slapped the barrel of her chest and the mare obligingly backed up, letting him enter the stable. Tarot moved to one side, saying nothing, but watching him carefully, grey eyes shadowed in an expressionless face.

Cal too stayed silent. Now the moment had come, he was no longer sure what he wanted to say to the woman. He sat on the wide stone lip of the manger, suddenly feeling the exertion of walking down here, and gestured for her to carry on grooming. After a moment's hesitation, she did so, humming under her breath as she swept the brush along the gleaming chestnut coat. Cal watched her for a few minutes.

'She's looking well,' he ventured.

'She is a good horse.'

Tarot didn't lift her head from where she was brushing out the long, white feathers. Taking advantage of her turned back, Cal climbed carefully to his feet, keeping a grip on the manger, until he was sure he had his balance. He ducked under the mare's drooping head and ran his good hand down the Duchess' leg, picking up one massive hoof. It was spotless, the frog picked clean and oiled.

Tarot said nothing, but he could feel her eyes on him as he walked round the mare, running his hand over her coat and checking that the itchy spots on her girth and withers had been brushed out properly, before going back to his perch on the manger.

'My sister says I owe you my life.'

Tarot shook her head. 'The healer here would have saved you.'

'But he didn't need to, did he?' Cal couldn't have said why that galled him so much. He should have been pleased that Tarot had been able to help. After all, he was the one who had agreed to her travelling with them. 'You took care of that.'

The way he said it, it was almost an accusation but, if Tarot took offence at his tone, she chose not to show it.

'I did what was necessary.' A dismissive shrug of the thin shoulders. 'Any healer would have done the same.'

It was a reasonable enough answer, but Cal wanted more from her than that. He tried again. 'You saved my life in the fight. Why?'

That, at least, made her pause. She looked up at him, head cocked to one side; a pied wagtail now, rather than a crow. But, if his question had elicited a reaction, it did not bring him an answer.

Instead she threw a question back at him. 'Why did you save Ilya?'

'That's a stupid thing to ask; he's my friend.'

'Indeed.' She set down the body brush and reached for a stiff bristled dandy, setting to work on the mare's tail.

Cal pressed her. 'That trap wasn't set for you. You could have walked away.'

The brushstrokes did not falter. 'I did not say it was I who needed protection.'

Cal sighed. He shifted further along the manger, until he could lean his back against the wall, then tilted his head back onto the rough bricks and closed his eyes. He simply wasn't up to this level of verbal fencing; not at the moment. His arm was starting to throb, and he wondered briefly what his chances were of getting the manor's healer to give him something for the pain, without Kat finding out. Slim to non-existent, he reckoned. Or, to put it another way, about as likely as getting a straight answer out of Tarot if he didn't ask her directly.

He listened to the soft sound of Tarot's humming as she continued to sweep the brush through the mare's tail, and the odd rustle as the Duchess shifted her feet in the straw. It seemed there was no other way for it. Straightening up again, he took a deep breath and plunged in. 'Is that what you do: protect people?'

He had an image of the black-clad figure materialising during a moment of crisis, then fading into the background once everything had been resolved. A few days ago, the idea would have made him laugh. Somehow it seemed quite reasonable now.

'If it is the right thing to do.' Another sweep of the brush, then she added, 'The world has more need of you and your troupe than it has for those brigands.'

So that was what it came down to, was it? She had seen trouble lurking in the cards, and had judged them worthy of her intervention.

'Why didn't you just tell us to avoid the forest road?'

'It doesn't work like that.'

No, he thought, *it wouldn't*. Not for Tarot. For some reason that amused him. But if that were all she had wanted to do, why was she still here? Why hadn't she simply taken their thanks and her share of the bounty, and gone? 'What do you really want, Tarot?'

The brushstrokes stopped, and the lanky fortune teller straightened up. For a long moment she didn't speak, and Cal was reminded of their first meeting. Had it really been just a week ago? Now, as then, he had the impression she was searching for the right words, weighing up what she would and would not say, as though much rested upon the choice, and the wrong one would shatter all her hopes.

'I want to travel with you and your troupe.'

'Why would you be willing to pay for the privilege of travelling with us when even I don't know where we'll go next?' he said, choosing to misunderstand her, forcing her to spell out what she wanted, just as he had been forced to ask her.

Her lips tightened briefly, the Tarot equivalent of a scowl, and she shook her head.

'I want to *join* your troupe,' she said. There was no hint of emotion in her voice. She would not cajole or plead and, if he said no, Cal knew she would not try to force the issue. Yet something told him this was no passing fancy.

So that was *what* she wanted. Perhaps the *why* would become clear in its own good time, if he trusted to Lady Fortune. It was not always easy, but sometimes it was all a traveller could do.

'Well, it seems everyone else wants you along,' he said, sourly.

'But you don't?'

Cal looked at her. He didn't answer, couldn't answer, if truth be told. Couldn't bring himself to give voice to the mix of emotions that prospect raised in him. After a second he stood and left the stable without saying anything. But the dusty sunlight glinted on the two silver coins he had left on the manger.

THE ONE-ARMED BANDIT

By Barbara Stevenson

The king stood at the top of the stairway, running his fingers along the alabaster bannister. The smoothness pleased him. He put a slippered foot on the intricately patterned Persian carpet and felt rich. He descended the stairs to the grand hall, allowing his footsteps to echo around the marble walls and felt powerful. He stood alone in the chamber and knew he was perfect.

Outside the palace, his subjects gathered in the market square, as they did every month, to await his decrees. His ministers huddled in their ermines on the balcony, slate tablets in hand, ready to implement his commands. The king counted to ten as he admired the Doric pillars, hand painted frescoes and carved ceiling. Satisfied, he tip-toed to the centre of the hall, where a jaded one-armed bandit was propped up with a wooden block. The slot for pennies was sealed over with duct tape, and a sign declaring "NOT IN USE" was pasted on the side, with the final "E" scratched out. The king reached for the lever, tightened his fingers round the metal, then jerked it down. The mechanism creaked and the symbols in the little windows spun round; not as fast as in previous years, but fast enough to allow the king to anticipate what would appear when they finished their revolutions.

Click, click, click.

Three new symbols, three new decrees.

As the king marched towards the balcony, he noticed a tiny gold thread hanging loose from the sleeve of his jacket.

That didn't please him.

The crowd nudged one another and hushed as their king appeared. He cleared his throat and announced the salutation: 'Greetings nonentities.' The audience applauded. 'Here are this month's decrees.' An expectant hush cut the air. 'One: the tax on citrus fruits will increase by ten percent.'

There were groans from parts of the square, changing to cheers when the royal guard made their presence known.

'Two: Tuesdays shall be public holidays.'

This time the celebration was genuine, especially among the schoolchildren. They were brought into line by a sharp blast of the headmistress' whistle.

'And finally, on the last day of the month, a tailor shall be led blindfolded to the market square and shot by firing squad.'

The sun darkened, and the birds stopped singing. A decree of such a nature had never been heard before, not even in the king's grandmother's day, and she had been an evil witch.

'The one-armed bandit has spoken,' the king finished. He looked around at his ministers and smiled. 'I think I'll have duck for dinner today.'

Claudius stood still as the townsfolk around him dispersed. The colour drained not only from his cheeks, but also from his suit. He felt under-dressed, naked. It took him a moment to realise someone was waving at him from across the square. Feebly, he lifted a hand to wave back. The other man approached him.

'What do you make of that, then?' Stanley asked.

'It's preposterous!' Claudius thrust the words out like a needle through leather.

'Which one of us will it be?' Stanley's voice implied it wasn't going to be him.

'We need to call an extraordinary general meeting of the

guild. This situation must be thoroughly thought through before a decision can be made.'

'Aye.' Stanley ran his tongue round the inside of his mouth. 'Thoroughly thought through.'

Claudius took a pocket diary, bound in kid-leather and edged in gold, from his inside pocket. He tweezed out the pencil lodged in the spine and chewed the end. 'Where and when should we meet?'

'We're here now.'

'But it isn't in my diary. We need time to come up with a solution to our dilemma.'

'I've come up with one already,' Stanley said with a grin, that was nipped by Claudius' frown.

'I am the king's personal tailor,' Claudius reminded him. 'I create bespoke clothing for lords and ladies. My shirts dance into shape on the chest. My jackets are sewn with...'

'Stardust; aye, I know. Meanwhile, I employ half the town to churn out shirts and trousers for the rest of the population. Who do you think would be more missed?'

'I see you don't wear your factory suits, but we needn't argue about it. I suggest we meet this evening, in the Hat and Rabbit at half past seven.'

'Eight o'clock,' Stanley replied. 'And it's your round.'

The inn was crammed to bursting, thanks to a live screening of the lettuce growing championship final. Lettuces brought Claudius out in suppurative boils. His skin tingled at the mention of the word and he feared sitting would be a delicate manoeuvre. Stanley relieved two tourists of their seats while Claudius bought the drinks. He shifted his way past the revellers, carrying the glasses close to his chest. On screen, the kingdom champion produced his lilac cos and the spectators rose to cheer. The pumping fist of a local farmer nudged Claudius' elbow, sending his Advocaat and lime dribbling down his silk shirt.

'You clot! I'll see you dunked in the frog pond for that.'

The farmer stammered an apology, wiping at Claudius' shirt with his stained neckerchief. Claudius pushed him aside. The rest of the lettuce fans in the room parted to allow him to pass.

'You shouldn't get uptight,' Stanley advised, as Claudius set his beer on the table. 'You only have thirty days to live. Enjoy them.'

'What makes you think I will be the one to be shot?'

'I have a wife and five children. Nobody cares about you.'

'That isn't true, there's ... and ... perhaps ...' Claudius counted on his fingers, gave up and sulked.

'When the time comes, can I have your sewing machine?' Stanley asked.

'Certainly not.'

'There you go, being peevish again.'

Claudius sat in silence, sipping the remains of his drink. Stanley gulped his down and waited for Claudius to fetch another. 'If you've nothing further to offer, I'll be on my way,' he said, when the refill didn't materialise.

'Wait!' Claudius jumped in his chair. 'I have an idea. I believe it is time we allowed a new member into our sacred guild of tailors.'

'Oh? You have always argued for a closed shop, to safeguard our stitching.'

'In the past, yes, that has served us well; but the town has grown, and we are getting older. There is work for another tailor.'

'Do you have somebody in mind?' Stanley probed.

'No-one in particular, but there would be certain requirements.'

'Such as?'

'Someone from outside the kingdom.'

'Unfamiliar with the king's decree,' Stanley qualified.

'Someone whose language skills aren't sharp.'

'So they won't understand.'

'Someone with little money, and a family that need providing for,' Claudius continued.

'A desperate man, who will agree to anything to help his family.'

'Exactly.'

'You are inviting someone into our guild to be shot,' Stanley clarified.

'I didn't make the decree. Besides, can you be sure the king will choose *me*?'

Stanley ran his tongue round his mouth. It was an annoying habit that Claudius deplored, but he kept this opinion to himself. Stanley gave a nod and clicked his empty glass against Claudius'. 'Proposal seconded.'

'Good.' Claudius smiled. 'I suggest we take a trip to the refugee camp tomorrow to select a suitable candidate.'

'You can go on your own. I'll be busy in my vegetable plot, laying a long-acting nerve poison to eliminate snails.'

The train line terminated a mile from the refugee camp. There were no buses or cabs. There was no need for them. The unmanned railway station was the only building in sight.

'The camp is that way, sir,' the guard informed Claudius, before blowing his whistle and jumping back on the train.

The engine wheeled out of sight, leaving an eerie silence. Claudius felt like he was in a vacuum on a distant star. He stumbled along a dust track towards the camp, with vultures circling overhead. He thought he could make out the silhouettes of coyotes. Red signs warned him he was approaching a restricted zone and he was stopped by armed soldiers who demanded to see his papers. Ahead of him, Claudius could see a twenty foot high stone wall, trimmed with barbed wire. When he reached the gate, a notice informed him the wire was electrified.

'What business have you here?' the sergeant at the entrance demanded.

Claudius pulled himself up and puffed out his chest. 'I am the king's tailor. I have come to find an apprentice.'

The sergeant and his junior officer burst out laughing. Even the Rottweiler on its flimsy lead rolled on the ground, kicking its legs. Claudius guessed that news of the king's decree had reached their barren outpost.

'Do you have the king's permission?' the sergeant asked.

'I have a proclamation from the President of the Sacred Guild of Tailors, ratified by the Vice-president, Secretary and Treasurer of the aforementioned guild.' Claudius produced a scroll from his travelling bag.

The sergeant scrutinised the writing.

'This is signed by yourself and someone called ... Hanley? Manley?'

'Stanley. Stanley Sewman: the Vice-president and Secretary.'

The sergeant flicked his eyes back and forth across the paper, then examined Claudius, before relenting. 'Very well. Wait here while we find suitable candidates.'

Claudius wobbled on a rickety stool in the guardhouse and smiled at the junior officer, as the man oiled his rifle. 'Is there much call for that?' he asked, nodding towards the gun.

The man ignored his question. In the yard, Claudius could hear shouting. A whip was cracked, and he lost his balance and fell off the stool. He got to his feet and was arranging the folds of his tweed jacket when the sergeant returned, pulling a chain. Three men in filthy yellow tunics were attached to it by ropes, the ends tied round their wrists. The sergeant stopped and gave the chain a tug, knocking the three weak-legged men to their knees.

'These are refugees, not criminals, yes?' Claudius said. 'I wouldn't want to enrol anyone of a dubious character into our sacred guild.'

'Introduce yourselves to the King's Master Tailor,' the sergeant growled.

Two of the men cowered and were silent, but the third tutted and reached over with his bound hands to brush a flake of dust from the sleeve of Claudius' jacket. 'Much better,' he said.

'Who are you?' Claudius asked.

'I am not a criminal, sir. I too am a master tailor, forced to leave my home and position, because of war. I once made gowns for my Empress and dancing suits for her consort that could waltz on their own. I was a rich man, an important man, but I spent my money getting here. I am no longer honoured.' He raised his roughened hands to inspect them. 'My fingers are swollen and my palms are cracked, but I can still sew.'

'I imagine you will find standards in this kingdom much higher than in your own,' Claudius replied, 'but you will do. Do you have a family?'

'A wife and three children. They are the reason I left my homeland.'

'Excellent,' Claudius smiled. 'Do you have a name?'

Claudius marked another day off his calendar as he prepared for bed. There were only twenty days left in the month. The new tailor, Aslo, was settling in well. So well, he had been asked to make a shirt for the king. His children were invited to play with those at the royal court. Claudius couldn't sleep. His plan wasn't working. He was being usurped. There was only one thing left to do: a drastic measure, but a necessary one. That night, Claudius broke open his piggy bank, packed his valuables in a travelling case, and fled the kingdom.

'We don't need tailors here,' he was told, when he applied

for a work permit in the next country. 'In fact, we're overrun by them. Citizens from your kingdom who can't get into your guild; funny that.'

'I have money,' Claudius offered.

'Give me a thousand and I'll see what I can do.'

Claudius counted out the notes, but a permit didn't arrive. He waited in a five-star hotel, then a bed and breakfast establishment, and finally a hostel, before realising he should move on. In the next kingdom, he was requested to attend an interview with the employment official's trainee assistant. The meeting was in a dimly lit basement. Claudius took a seat opposite a puffy-faced woman wearing a plain, cotton tunic. His gaze was drawn to her elaborate headwear. To call it a hat would have been a criminal injustice. The brim accommodated a model train that whirled round a miniature domed city, constructed from chocolate and candies. At every puff of steam, the delicious fragrance of spring rosebuds wafted across the desk.

'It's a grade three,' the woman explained. 'When I finish my training, I'll earn a grade five: an ocean liner with the aroma of sandalwood.'

'Delightful.' Claudius clasped his knees. 'About my work permit ...'

The woman shuffled a pile of papers. 'Occupation?'

'I'm a tailor.'

'You make tails?' The woman rubbed her chin. 'A new fashion for us, but I can see it catching on. Wagging tails when we're happy, swishing tails when we're cross. Luxury furs or rat tails for the unemployed.' She stared at Claudius.

'I make clothes,' Claudius corrected her.

'Not tails?' The train on the hat screeched to a halt. Sparks flew from the rails.

'Tailcoats, perhaps,' Claudius offered. If the woman had had a tail, it would have been swishing. 'But mainly shirts, jackets and trousers.'

'We have no need of those.'

'Tunics?'

'Good afternoon,' she said, dismissing him with a puff of steam from the train.

It was still morning. Claudius was tempted to break off the ginger snap, model clock tower on her hat to show her. Although he was partial to these biscuits, he didn't feel that would help his case.

He paid two hundred coins to enter the neighbouring state, but no-one required a tailor there either. When his money ran out, he sold his fine clothes. He walked the streets dressed in rags and bit his nails to temper the pangs of hunger. Children threw mud at him and shouted names. He wasn't familiar with the language, but he knew what they were calling him. It came as a relief when he was arrested as a vagabond and thrown in the dungeons.

'We don't want parasites here,' the jailer chaffed. 'You will be deported back to your own country.'

A number was painted on a board and hung round Claudius' neck. His head was shaved and he was hustled into a cattle truck that bumped its way back to his homeland, passing the refugee camp with its wailing inmates.

'Hurry up, or you'll miss supper.' The prison guard jabbed Claudius in the backside with his bayonet, to speed him into an overcrowded cell that smelt of urine. 'It's leftover lettuce from the championship final. A tad soggy, but the slime can be wiped off. If you're lucky, you'll find a snail.'

Claudius scratched his itchy scalp. 'Thank you, but I'm not hungry.' His stomach gurgled. 'What day is it?'

'It's the last day of the month.' The guard clicked his tongue to make a noise like bullets popping from a gun. 'I'm to be part of the firing squad in the market square this evening. I've polished my rifle already.'

'Congratulations.' Claudius swallowed. 'And has a tailor been selected?'

'Certainly,' the man answered. 'The Sacred Guild of Tailors has nominated ... you.'

'But I'm the President of the Guild.'

'Then you have made a noble gesture, sir.'

Claudius' legs were shaking, but he pictured himself shoving Stanley's head down into a tub of tacking pins and managed to stand his ground. 'Would I be allowed a last request?'

'Why, of course.'

'I would like to speak with the king, before my execution.'

'It would be difficult speaking to him afterward,' the guard joked. Claudius didn't laugh.

The king agreed to this request and Claudius was brought before him in his mouldy rags, stinking of the rat-ridden dungeon. He couldn't help noticing how sharp the king's suit was, exquisitely tailored with not a stitch visible. It wasn't one of his suits. He fell on his knees before the king.

'Majesty, please, I have done nothing wrong. I haven't stolen or killed. I have always paid my taxes.'

'It's nothing personal, Claudius, although the last suit you made for me did have a loose thread.'

'If you are unhappy with my work, allow me to make you a wonderful new suit, better than anything you have worn before. Sumptuous silk, hand-dyed by the craftswomen in the mountains, with the threads spun by silver spiders. The buttons will be crafted from pink topaz, set in white gold.'

'Hmm.' The king pondered the suggestion.

'And a hat,' Claudius added.

'I'm afraid the one-armed bandit has spoken.'

'It is a mere gaming machine.'

'And what is life, but a game. Sometimes you win, sometimes you lose. Start changing the rules and it leads to anarchy. Take him away, guards.'

'Nobody wins against the one-armed bandit,' Claudius

muttered, and was biffed on the head by the butt of the guard's gun.

A crowd gathered in the market square. Claudius could hear their excited murmuring, as he was led blindfolded to the execution spot. His bladder was weak and he feared making a fool of himself, even in death.

'Halt.'

Claudius stopped. He felt strong arms on his shoulder and he was twirled round. He heard the shuffling of footsteps as the soldiers took their positions. The crowd was quiet. Claudius' teeth chattered.

'Ready. Aim. Fire.'

Claudius heard the blast of the guns discharging and fell to the ground. Apart from skinning his knees on the stone, there wasn't the expected pain. He was alive. He felt his chest for gunshot wounds and blood. The blindfold was whipped from his head, and the king was standing before him.

'Stop sniveling, nincompoop; they fired blanks.'

'Blanks? I see. Can I go home now, please?' Claudius' bottom lip quivered as he spoke.

'Go home and get to work. I want that suit you promised me ready by Friday, or you'll be dunked in the frog pond.'

'Th ... this Friday? I may need help.'

The king was walking off. Claudius took his lack of a refusal to mean he was in agreement. A picture of the fortress and its desperate inhabitants flashed into his head. He would need lots of help, he decided. It really was time the guild opened its door to new members.

The king returned to his palace, and the next day descended to the great hall to pull the lever of the one-armed bandit. The symbols wheeled round and stopped where fate intended. The king strode to the balcony to address his subjects.

'Greetings, my loyal servants. Here are this month's decrees. One: bars will be closed on Mondays until further notice. Two: church bells will be rung at four o'clock every morning. Three: all snails shall have their shells painted gold, and will be given the freedom of the kingdom. Anyone hurting them, even unwittingly, will be thrown in the dungeons for a month.'

In the crowd, Claudius looked over to Stanley and gave a wry smile.

DARK FANTASY

SUGAR CUBE

BY JOSEPH DEGAND

While visiting my grandparents for a long weekend about four-and-a-half years ago, my Grandpa and I sat in their antiquated study chatting. He was reclined in his favourite blue velvet chair and me on the fairly worn-out, double-cushioned, IKEA loveseat I used to nap on as kid – until my legs were too long to fit anymore.

We talked about it all that evening – from life and death to everything in-between. Our conversation lasted for hours, but as the night went on, I noticed his demeanor gradually become quite sullen and downtrodden. I thought it was simply him getting tired so, after several minutes of silence, you can imagine how confused I was when he suddenly asked me to grab his decades-old iPad and wireless keyboard from the desk across the room, and switch them on.

I walked across the study to fetch them, pressing the tablet's Power button as I plopped back down on the couch. Then we sat in silent anticipation, anxious to see whether it would finally be the night that the ancient device finally gave up the ghost. After minutes of excruciatingly slow loading, it finally got itself up and running, though – and that was when he asked if I'd mind lending an ear and transcribing a story for him.

'My fingers aren't what they used to be,' he said, 'with this damned arthritis.' He was an accountant, or key-cruncher as he liked to call it, before retiring in the fifties – a couple of years ahead of everything going computerised.

I obliged, but not before offering my holo-recorder for

the task. Why type when I could just record him in 3D? He politely declined, though, mainly because he did his very best to keep most modern technology at arm's length. He much preferred the bulky tablets and manual gadgets from back in his heyday during the mid-2000s.

Before starting, he said, 'I've never told this tale to another soul – at least not the whole thing – and I don't expect you to either. Promise me you won't share what I'm about to tell you with anyone, not even your parents, until your Grandma and me are both long gone.'

Of course I swore to keep it between just the two of us.

A bit apprehensive at first, he started by enlightening me to the scandalous fact that there had been another woman in his life before Grandma; a woman he had been married to for two years and apparently loved very deeply. He spent a couple of minutes telling me about this lady, Sarah, who I wasn't even sure my parents or Grandma knew about.

I asked what had happened between them to cause a split in their marriage, especially since Grandpa wasn't the kind of guy to let a relationship fall to ruin without fighting until the very end.

That was when he began his tale – and I started typing.

It was the spring of 2010 and, in typical Wakefield fashion, we arrived at reception three minutes before checkout time at eleven.

Sarah urged me to wait in the car while she went inside to quickly return our lodge key to reception before we set off for another quick romp around a nearby lake, and then home. As she opened her door, a brisk wind blew in, tossing her long brown hair across her face. Before stepping out, she leant in close to whisper, 'I love you, Sugar Cube.'

In homage to one of our favourite films, I told her, 'I know,' with a smirk, then brushed her hair to the side. Our lips met once, twice, and a third time. She gently touched my face, and gave me a light tap on the cheek, as she pulled herself away.

'I'll be right back,' she said, shutting the door behind her. 'Don't miss me too much, Han.'

In a love-drunk stupor, I watched her make her way towards the Forest Lakes' main reception area. Its cedar log façade resembled something straight out of Thoreau's *Walden*.

I stared in adoration as she sauntered along, her hips swaying from side to side and her hair blowing free in the light spring breeze. She was only twenty-four years old at the time, and she wandered about so innocent and ignorant of her beauty, turning heads everywhere she went. Words really can't describe how much I loved watching her stroll through life. Being with her was a breath of fresh air – a beautiful and carefree spirit who'd decided I was the one she wanted to share the rest of her life with.

Watching her sent me into a daze and, without even realising it, I'd hunched over the steering wheel in a trance. Everything was frozen but her – my brown-haired angel. As she walked, her vibrant blue sundress contrasted perfectly with the earthy green landscape and brownish-red exterior of the building. Perfect in every way, she was mine and I loved her.

The first set of automatic doors leading into the reception broke me from her spell as she slipped inside. Before stepping through the next set, she stopped, beaming, and blew me kiss as the first doors closed behind her. I slouched back into my seat with a foolish grin on my face, and waited.

I reclined my seat and replayed the lovely long weekend we'd just spent in Warton-on-Carn. Majestic sights, long walks and unbridled romance – a much-needed getaway to break up the monotony of everyday life that the two of us were always grumbling about. My mind raced thinking about how the first two years of married life had flown by, while also wondering what the future might have in store for us. Where would we be a year from now? In five? Twenty? How many kids would we have? What kind of place would we be calling home? The things all couples try to plan and guess, but can rarely foresee.

Needless to say, I lost track of time as my mind wandered, but was instantly pulled back to reality when I glanced at the car's digital display and saw that it was half-past-eleven. Had I really been daydreaming for half an hour? More importantly, where was Sarah?

I assumed she'd just been drawn into a conversation with one of the receptionists, or had to use the ladies' room, so I sent her a text message to check she was okay. After five more minutes passed without a reply, a storm of worry hit me. I locked the car and hurried to find out where she was.

Once inside reception, I spun round in a desperate attempt to spot her. No sign, so I approached the plump blonde behind the front desk. Panic was setting in, and my heart was pounding. 'Excuse me ...' I said, glancing at the badge on her chest, '... Beckie, but have you seen my wife?' I was still trying to catch my breath. 'She came in here over half an hour ago to check us out, but never came back to the car.'

She looked at me over her red-rimmed spectacles. 'We were quite busy with checkouts at eleven. What does she look like?'

'Brown hair, brown eyes, about my height. She's young, in her mid-twenties. Had a flowery blue dress on ...'

She interrupted, 'I'm sorry, but I don't recall seeing her.'

Increasingly desperate and short-tempered, I shouted, 'What do you mean you haven't seen her? You're the only person behind that goddamned desk – you must have seen her!' I turned and pointed. 'I watched her walk through those doors right over there!'

Despite my outburst, she remained quite calm. 'And I'm

telling *you*, sir, that I haven't seen anyone matching that description. I'm sorry you can't find your wife, but if you give me your name, I can look to see if she checked out.'

Impatiently, I answered, 'Tom. Tom Wakefield.'

She typed, clicked and typed some more, before showing me her screen. 'I'm sorry, Mr Wakefield, but you're still checked in. Your wife wasn't here.'

I slammed a clenched fist onto the counter. 'Yes, she was! I'm not making this up, lady!' I told her in a strange kind of hushed shout.

She pointed at the screen again and repeated that we were still checked in, and she hadn't seen Sarah. 'I'm sorry you've misplaced your wife, sir, but I really don't know what else to I can do.' Her tone was becoming terse and slightly condescending, so much so that I had to stop myself from reaching over the desk and shaking her.

'Where's the manager?' I demanded. 'I want to speak to whoever's in charge.'

Peering at me, she slid ungracefully from her chair. 'I'll be right back, sir,' she said, as she wobbled around the corner to find her supervisor.

By that point, everyone else in reception had frozen in a state of nosy interest, focusing their attention on me. I did my best to ignore the couple near the entrance, who were staring and whispering, as well as the woman shaking her head and throwing a dirty look my way as she led her little girl into the restroom. I did, however, make accidental eye contact with one of the two burly resort security guards whose interest I'd also piqued with my tirade.

I stood impatiently, unable to shake the mounting feeling that my wife was slipping further and further away with every passing second. After a minute or so of waiting, I slammed a heavy fist onto the marble counter again and shouted, 'Where's the damned manager?'

Seconds later, a respectable-looking man shuffled

around the corner, followed by the unhelpful blonde. 'How can I help you, sir?' His badge told me his name was Simon Davies and that he was Assistant Manager.

Not bothering to question his snooty tone, I jumped straight into explaining the situation again. Luckily for me, it turned out I was not mistaken about Sarah's head-turning beauty because, after describing her in as much detail as I could, he thought he may have seen her come in and walk straight into the ladies' restroom while he was monitoring the reception's live security feed.

'We were busy at the time, though,' he said, 'so I came out to help Beckie, and can't be sure whether …'

I suspected his next words were going to be that he hadn't seen her come out again, so I didn't stand around to listen. Instead, I stormed to the ladies' toilets and shoved the door open, terrifying the judgmental mother from earlier, who was now helping her daughter wash her hands. The little girl shrieked as her mother scooped her up and shoved past me, out the door.

I ignored her and stood there, shouting Sarah's name over and over, hoping with all my heart she would reply in her soft, sweet voice. No such luck. I slammed open each of the stall doors, before desperately checking for any windows or other doors she could have left through. Finally, in a delirious yet desperate attempt to find an alternative exit, I ran my hands along the walls, hoping to discover some sort of hidden passage she might have stumbled across. No joy again, though.

Immersed in my search, my concentration was broken when I heard a muted shout from outside the restroom. Seconds later, the two security guards stormed in, wrapped their arms around mine and manhandled me out the loo door and onto a chair in the lobby. I noticed that the entire area had been cleared of people. Not even the manager and receptionist were in sight.

'Someone call the police!' I shouted. 'I need the police!' Unsurprisingly, someone *had* already rung them – something I realised when I caught a glimpse of blue lights dancing on the ceiling above the main entrance.

Desperate to break free and continue my search for Sarah, I tried shrugging my arms from the guards' strong grips. It didn't work and, despite my shouting and pleading, I was forced back down, unable to shake the thought that I might never have another chance to kiss my wife and tell her I love her.

I felt my sanity slipping away with every second that passed, but pulled myself together as the doors beside me opened and the manager walked through them, accompanied by three Warton-on-Carn officers.

I tried to stand, but was again shoved back down. The manager pointed at me. 'This is him – the one who frightened our guests and shouted at Beckie here, before forcing himself into the womens' room while a little girl and her mother were inside.'

As he wrapped up his testimony, I noticed each of the officers shoot glances at me. The chief inspector thanked the manager and finally directed his attention to me.

'Good morning, Mr Wakefield,' he said, glancing down at his watch. 'Or should I say afternoon now? Anyway, I'm Chief Inspector Hughes, and this is Officer Thorpe and Officer Nichols. Based on what Mr. Davies here said, you've caused quite a commotion. What seems to be the trouble?'

I explained everything again. They listened intently, scanning the ceiling when I mentioned how the manager said he'd seen Sarah on the security footage. When I finished my story, Chief Inspector Hughes asked the manager about the black globes scattered above us.

'Could I have a look at the footage from this morning, Mr Davies? Say from 10am to present?'

'Sure, the equipment is right round the back of reception,

in the office,' he answered.

Hughes excused himself, but not before requesting that Officers Thorpe and Nichols keep an eye on me until he was back, indirectly dismissing Forest Lakes' overbearing guards. My relief must have shown, because Hughes gave me a slight nod after issuing the order.

For a third time, I was left to wait, feeling completely hopeless. Knowing I had two officers watching over me now, I did my best to remain patient. Soon, bittersweet thoughts of Sarah started sputtering through my head, as I relived all the happy times she and I had shared. Those memories came to a sudden halt though, as the harsh realisation that I may never see her again hit me like a ton of bricks once more. That was it – my emotions finally got the better of me, and I let out a piercing cry that frightened the pants off the two officers beside me.

Tears fell uncontrollably as I wept Sarah's name, leaving Thorpe and Nichols unsure what to do. They did their best to calm me, but my grief was too much for them. The most they could do was pat my back and offer a handkerchief.

By the time Inspector Hughes and Davies reemerged, I had regained my composure for the most part, and was sat slouched, with my head hanging down in my hands.

Hughes asked, 'Mr Wakefield, are you all right? Do you need a couple more minutes?'

I lifted my head. 'No, I'm … I'm okay.'

'Right, well, what I saw on camera was most interesting,' he said. 'Everything I saw seems to validate both yours and Mr Davies's stories.'

He confirmed that the resort's security footage showed Sarah and me parking in front of the building, as well as Sarah making her way inside. And, most importantly, it showed her entering the women's toilets, but not coming back out.

'If you don't mind, Mr Wakefield, I'd like to ask you a few

questions in private,' said Hughes, before asking Davies if there was a place he and I could chat.

By that time, more police had arrived and were conducting what turned out to be a fruitless top-to-bottom search of the building, particularly the restrooms. Meanwhile, Davies led me and Hughes into his office with the CCTV screens.

'Please let me know if I can be of any further help,' he said, smiling at Hughes, before throwing a harsh glance at me as he shut the door behind him.

'This all must be very confusing and difficult for you, Mr Wakefield,' started Hughes.

After a minute or two of one-sided chatter, he began asking his questions.

Were Sarah and I happy in our marriage?

Of course we were. Years of managing a long distance relationship adds a certain level of appreciation for one's partner.

Was she seeing anyone else that I was aware of?

No.

Was I seeing anyone else that she could have found out about?

No.

Had we recently had any disagreements or arguments?

Possibly. If the question was whether either of us recently had a go at the other for not wiping the counter or leaving dirty laundry on the floor, then yes. But, if it was a question of whether we had recently fought about anything that would make her want to leave, then no.

After answering all of his questions, Hughes stood up, saying I'd most likely have to be interviewed again formally a bit later, so that my statement could be properly recorded for future reference. I agreed but, before he had a chance to open the door and lead us back into the lobby, I asked if there was any chance I could have a look at the security footage from earlier. He could tell the day's events had taken their toll on me, so he reluctantly agreed.

Before pressing play, he checked one last time: 'Are you sure you want to watch?'

I nodded, and my heart instantly sank as I watched Sarah walk into the lobby, straight to the loo. He clicked fast-forward, pointing out how no one went in or out of the door again until the mother and daughter that I had frightened.

'You also mentioned there was footage of us in the parking lot. Could I see that too?' I asked.

He obliged, but seconds after watching us kiss for the last time, I had to excuse myself. Hughes gave me a minute alone, before stepping outside the office to ask if there was anyone I needed to call about all this – perhaps Sarah's parents.

'I … I don't think I can do it, Inspector. What do I say? What do I tell them?'

He could tell I was in no state to ring them, so he offered to do it. Within hours, they arrived and met me at the police station. They were both as confused and distraught as I was, but it still helped having them there for comfort and company.

That night, I slipped into an uneasy sleep at the B&B that Sarah's parents and I had booked into. The next morning, during those first few groggy seconds of waking, I'd forgotten what had happened the day before and was confused when Sarah wasn't by my side. After coming to and getting up, I drifted through the rest of the day, fully expecting her to return with a perfectly logical excuse for her disappearance and all the madness it had caused. But she never did.

As the days passed, each hour started to feel more like two, and I felt little pieces of me dying with each sunset. And no matter how often Sarah's parents and I enquired with Inspector Hughes, there never seemed to be any progress.

Hailing from another country, and without any close friends or family nearby, apart from Sarah's parents, the grasp of loneliness grew tighter with each night I spent sleeping on my own. Looking back, I regret the coldness I showed my concerned connections overseas, but their calls felt contrived and empty at the time, especially their constant enquiries about whether I was okay and if there was any new information. So much so that I gave up answering my phone and switching my computer on because, every time I had to answer those questions, I felt forced to put on a façade of calm and strength that wasn't anywhere near true to how I was actually feeling.

On top of everything, local reporters had somehow been made aware of the case, but thankfully kept their distance from me and my in-laws, mainly due to Inspector Hughes' thoughtful intervention.

At the end of one particularly long week spent waiting for news that never arrived, Sarah's parents realised they'd put their lives on hold for several weeks and decided there was nothing more they could do to move the investigation forward. Halfheartedly, they decided it would be healthier to return home until they were needed, or new word came through from Hughes.

'You should really join us, Tom,' said Sarah's mom. 'There's nothing else we can do here. I know this is hard to hear because it's incredibly hard for me to say, but it might be best for us all to start trying to carry on without her. Plus, Inspector Hughes promised he'd be in touch if he finds anything new.'

Despite their best efforts, I graciously declined, mainly because I couldn't bring myself to leave Warton-on-Carn without my wife. So they left, and two days after they did, reality hit me hard.

I realised I either had to leave town, or commit to staying for the foreseeable future. Despite the lack of new information, I let emotion get the better of me and decided it wouldn't feel right to leave and try moving on with life while Sarah was missing. So I travelled home to gather some belongings for my indefinite stay in Warton-on-Carn. While there, I also tied up some loose ends, like resigning from my job at the accountancy firm I was working for at the time.

Being inside the house without Sarah was both heartbreaking and unsettling. While packing, I slipped into a bout of sorrow in our bedroom while looking at her dresser and the beautiful clutter scattered on top of it. Somehow, I was able to snap myself out of it long enough to throw a load of clothes and personal effects into a huge duffel bag, set up several direct debits for all our outgoings, and leave our home behind until Sarah and I could return to it together.

From then, my days in Warton-on-Carn dragged on in an endless haze. Not only had I set aside my knack for key-crunching in favour of part-time work as a bar assistant, but I also spent most of my free time trying to piece together the mystery of my missing wife. Despite my best efforts though, I couldn't find anything in Warton-on-Carn's archived newspapers to suggest that something like this might have happened before. No missing persons, strange disappearances or unsolved mysteries. Even when I stretched for implausible explanations, research on the town itself didn't turn up anything out of the ordinary, like it being situated over the top of a prehistoric praying ground, Pagan place of sacrifice or anything else occult or supernatural. In fact, most people knew it as being one of the quaintest places in the country and a getaway for many famous novelists, artists and poets.

On top of my research, I was also making an effort to visit Forest Lakes on a daily basis, for no other reason than to search for any clue or answer the police might have missed. This obsessive compulsive routine came to an abrupt end though, following an alcohol-fuelled night that ended with me berating the resort's reception staff with a diverse mix of profanity and accusations, followed by a detailed pledge of retribution and violence. Needless to say, the police were called and I was officially banned from setting foot on Forest Lakes property again.

In fact, that episode ended up landing me in jail for the night, resulting in my first face-to-face conversation with Inspector Hughes for nearly two months. Upon finding out I'd been brought in for being drunk and disorderly, he moved me into a stuffy white interrogation room.

'What're you doing, Tom?' he asked, in disgust at the state I was in. 'This,' he said, gesturing with disdain at me, 'isn't helping anything. Telling the folks over at Forest Lakes you would - and I quote – "cut each and every one of them to pieces if they didn't give your wife back". Really? That's not gonna help bring Sarah back, is it, Tom?'

'You son-of-a-bitch, don't you dare say her name. You … you don't have the right,' I slurred. 'Two months! Two months, you've been searching for her, and where has it gotten you? Where has it gotten me? Nowhere! I'd sooner die than leave things to you and your useless department! You're all no good pigs, as far as I'm concerned!'

That was the straw that broke the camel's back, and Hughes's demeanor changed in an instant from empathetic to irate. 'You listen hear, Wakefield,' he shouted. 'We've done everything in our power to find your wife – but she's gone! She's nowhere to be found! You need to move on … get out of Warton-on-Carn. You're not helping the case, and you're not helping yourself by being here.'

I shouted, 'Leave? Leave? What kind of man do you think I am? What kind of husband do you think I am?' As I spoke, my rage slowly turned to tears, as I realised Hughes was right. 'I … I can't go. I can't leave her, Hughes. I can't …'

Hughes lightened a bit. 'Fine, Tom; do as you please. Stay if you want. But I swear to God, if I see your face back here, or hear about you doing anything out of line, I'll have you thrown back in jail without hesitation.' He stood up and ordered me to be put back in the cell until I sobered up.

They released me the next morning and, ironically, from that point on, the weeks kept passing, but my drive to find Sarah slowly faded thanks to the solace I was finding in a nightly bottle of gin. All the while, hopelessness and despair festered inside of me to such a degree that not only had I been considering ending my search, but also my miserable life.

Four more slow months passed, as the demons of loneliness remained my worst enemies, but also my best friends. I stopped working. I was slowly draining mine and Sarah's life savings. And I was becoming ever more distant to my family and friends, not even bothering to answer calls from Sarah's parents anymore.

One morning, after a particularly low evening that ended in two bottles of gin polished off, and me in the bath with a sharp bread knife resting against my wrist, I was brought back to consciousness by the incessant chirping of my phone. I ignored it as best I could but, after five minutes of relentless on-and-off ringing, I mustered enough strength to pull my wrinkled body out of the tub to check who was calling me after months of isolation.

It was Hughes, and what he told me was enough to sober me up in an instant. 'Tom, it's Inspector Hughes. I've got some news about Sarah's case,' he said. 'Can you make it to the station as soon as possible?'

'I … uh … I'll be there right away,' I said, and hung up.

Despite my throbbing head, and the small bleeding cut on my arm from the knife I couldn't find the courage to fully dig into myself, I dried off, wrapped my wound, threw on some clothes, and left for the police station. Since her disappearance, I'd been fighting to keep Sarah's memory alive in my head but, as it so often does to people, time, and gin, had faded it. But now, it all came flooding back to me: her soft touch, her smile, her kiss. Despite Hughes not saying what sort of progress had been made, I was hopeful for the first time in six months. All sorts of thoughts filled my head. If Sarah was there, alive and well, what would I say to her? What would she say?

After a hurried half-mile walk, I made it to the station and explained to the officer on reception duty who I was and that Inspector Hughes had called me in. She encouraged me to sit and wait while she let him know I had arrived. But I had too much energy to sit, so I paced back and forth, until I saw Hughes walking towards me from down the hall.

'Hi Tom,' he said with a smile, extending a hand out to me – a greeting I hadn't been expecting, especially after our previous encounter. We shook hands and he said, 'Follow me,' before leading us into the same stuffy white room we had spoken in four months before. As we entered, I noticed an officer standing guard outside the room beside ours.

The room was incredibly warm, so I rolled up my sleeves, completely forgetting about my low point from the night before. Once we were both sat down, Hughes started things off by saying, 'Wow, Tom, you look like shit.' He glanced at my arm. 'Things okay?'

'I'm fine,' I said, quickly folding my sleeves back down. 'Just had a rough couple of nights, that's all. So, what's happened?'

Ignoring what he'd just seen, Hughes continued: 'Last night, we got a call from Forest Lakes at 3am, saying how a woman claiming to be your wife suddenly appeared in the lobby, but that she wouldn't speak any other words apart from, "I am Sarah Wakefield". So our guys rushed down to bring her into custody.

'The girl on reception said no guests had been into the reception building since midnight – but, three hours later, the door to the ladies' room slowly opened, and out stepped a woman in shock and trembling, eyes wide open, scaring the receptionist half to death.

'Now listen, Tom; believe me when I say not to get your

hopes up about this. I've met and tried speaking to the woman, and I'm extremely hesitant to believe it's your wife. A lead's a lead though, so I thought it best to call you so you could see for yourself, if only to discount her before we let her go. I really don't think …'

I interrupted: 'With all due respect, Inspector, could you just bring me in to see Sar … this woman?'

We stood and went out into the hall. Hughes dismissed the officer outside the door and said, 'Before I let you in, Tom, I can't help but stress how terribly confident I am that the woman inside *isn't* Sarah, and that you're only here to confirm that.'

'I'll be the judge,' I answered, as I turned the knob and made my way inside, nerves jangling and heart pounding. *Why would someone claim to be Sarah?* I wondered.

What I saw upon entering is still as shocking to me now as it was then. There, sat at the far end of a pale wood table, was a wrinkled old woman who looked to be at least ninety years old.

Confused and furious, I let some vulgarities slip out, and nearly stormed out of the room to berate Hughes for involving me in such a malicious joke – but then I caught a glimpse of the elderly stranger's eyes; despite the wrinkles and silvery white hair, there was something about those eyes. After several seconds of gazing deeply into them, my heart skipped a beat, and a feeling of indescribable dread fell over me as I noted their uncanny resemblance to Sarah's.

A look of shock filled the woman's face. She broke eye contact and winced, as she pushed her hands against the table in front of her to help her stand. Her knees and elbows seemed to shudder at the thought of supporting her fragile and seemingly undernourished frame, but she was soon upright and staring at me once again with those eyes.

'S-Sarah?' I asked.

An aged, but otherwise identical to my beloved's, smile

swept across the haggard woman's face. With a relieved sigh, she answered, 'Sugar Cube?' Her smile turned to a mangled expression of fear though, as she whispered, 'You've not aged. It's … it's been decades. So long. So painful. That place. That … place.' Her eyes broke away from mine, frantically scanning the room. She started breathing harder and faster with each passing second, before suddenly gasping for air and collapsing onto the table, never to wake again.

Grandpa finished his story by telling me that it had been exactly fifty-five years since the day he'd seen Sarah that one final time. Somehow, what happened that day had stayed out of the newspapers, leaving Sarah's disappearance as Warton-on-Carn's only ever unsolved mystery.

He noticed me struggling to transfer and backup his story to my iChip, so he paused for a couple of minutes. Once his tale was saved and secure, he carried on explaining how it had taken nearly a decade for him to come to terms with the fact that his wife would not be returning to him. However, with the help of family, friends and a highly regarded psychologist, he pulled through. Although he'd eventually moved on and started a family with Grandma here in Allerton, he still kept the old woman's ashes tucked away in his sock drawer. He said he loved Grandma no end, but that he sometimes found himself drifting away at the thought of the love he had lost and the horrors she must have endured during her disappearance – the likes of which he, and I, after hearing the story, can't begin to fathom.

Exhausted, he thanked me for listening and ended by telling me how her haunting final words still plagued his thoughts and dreams. Then he sighed, 'Sugar Cube,' as he slipped into a peaceful, final night's sleep.

THE NAUTILUS SHELL

By David Steven Malone

Ginny was almost four when life with her grandmother began. The cottage smelled of lemon soap and the garden made her sneeze. A river ran behind their home and filled the sea beyond the links. Perched upon the mantelpiece, above undying flames, a nautilus shell rocked; if you held it to your ear, you heard the ocean. The white coals in the hearth looked just like snow, until you picked one up. There were too many rooms for just two people.

On Ginny's fifth birthday, her grandmother called her to the garden; she was pinching withered strawberries and pushing them under the soil. Plum pollen coated Ginny's throat and choked her while she learned of death.

Mortality meant her mother was gone.

At night, Ginny listed all the ways she might die: burning, like a witch; drowning, like a sailor; shot, like a soldier; sick, like her mother; wine, like her uncle; crucified, like Christ; and time, like her grandfather.

She felt fire was the worst.

At school, Ginny learned to read and count and draw and write, but she never learned to swim. She was just past seven when her class went for lessons. Forbidden to leave the shallows, Ginny was left to float upon the surface. She hid her face beneath the water and listened to the dull torrent of blood in her ear; her red hair splayed the surface like October fern.

It hurt to open her eyes.

Water smothered the world away, like sleep.

One night, she skipped down to the beach and paddled out into the depths. A wave thrust her under, and she sank without a breath. Her lungs flooded with salt and blood.

Glaring through the seething blur, she kicked and grasped towards the moon, but her throat was wrung by swarming currents; her chest crushed by moonlit swells.

She writhed, inhaled, and drifted down.

All went cold and quiet; all was black, and still.

Ginny woke to falling tears:

'I thought I'd lost you. I thought you'd never wake.'

Her grandmother had grown so fragile.

This was not Ginny's room.

This was a hospital.

Ginny had lost three years to a coma.

Swimming was forbidden while her grandmother still lived, but the sea held no horror for Ginny; she still craved its solace. The diluted calm drawn from watching the river rise and fall and follow routine, ensured her grandmother's peace, but the dependable tide was tedious, and Ginny grew restless.

At night, she timed holding her breath with a minute sandglass, each turn a minute long. She saw the last grain fall on the second turn once; there never was a third.

She fainted and suffered the nightmares instead.

The mineshaft was a common torture.

The soot air bound her throat like gluten, while saltwater bled through the coal seam.

A candle burned down to death in her hand, while black silt swallowed her legs.

Her tongue swelled, and filled her mouth; her lips sealed in salivated tar. When the filth breached her nose, she thrashed and woke breathless in bed.

The loss of her teeth was a frequent concern.

Her left eyetooth wobbled over her tongue. She sucked it from her gum and spat it on her hand. It was long, and crooked, and yellow at the root. Her front teeth crumbled and her molars cracked. Her mouth bulged and her cheeks ripped, and the bloody shards drenched her lap.

White pain seared her chest and choked her soul. Wheezing and sweating, she clutched her jaw and wept.

One morning, she woke to find a rusted patch of blood seeping through her nightdress. Puberty meant her childhood was gone.

One year later, Ginny was almost orphaned.

The doctor's name was Turner. His pale white coat was a cape that splayed from his belly. 'Mrs. Greenwood has suffered a violent stroke,' he said. 'It's a miracle she's with us at all.'

Ginny's grandmother lay unconscious; her small frame billowed under the aid of an iron lung.

She seemed at peace.

'When will she wake?' asked Ginny.

'Only she can say.'

'Is she dreaming?'

'Sometimes.'

'I never dreamt in my coma.'

'You may not remember, but I promise you did.' The doctor produced a slim, grave smile, and left.

Ginny lay by her grandmother from dusk until dawn, mesmerised by the uncanny rhythm in her bosom.

The morning chorus heralded a nurse. 'I think you should go home and rest,' she said.

'I'm afraid to fall asleep' said Ginny.

The nurse offered a kind grin. 'Pray why, what's wrong?'

'Because I might die.'

'Sleep can't kill you, my love; we all must sleep to live.'

'When I sleep, I stop breathing. I suffocate 'til I wake.'

The nurse frowned: 'Apnea,' she whispered.

'What's that?' begged Ginny.

'An unconscious flaw; there's a sleep clinic here at the hospital. They might have a spare bed if you'd like to be tested?'

Ginny agreed and returned the next night.

The hospital bed was firm and thin. Ginny lay staring at the ceiling. Numerous machines with blinking lights flanked her slender limbs. On the windowsill, a nautilus shell rocked beneath a moonlight nimbus.

'These will record your heart, lungs, and brain,' said Dr Turner, offering his same grave smile. 'I want to monitor your body in sleep, especially while you dream.'

'Do your eyes move while you dream?' asked Ginny.

'Yes.'

'I saw my grandmother's eyes move today.'

'I told you she was dreaming.'

'Will she remember them?'

'I'm afraid I can't say for certain.'

The doctor left without saying goodnight.

She lay awake near an hour, and watched the golden second hand spin the oval clock-face opposite her bed; another hour passed before the pulsing machinery dimmed from notice, and one more still before she forgot the groping wires feeding on her body.

All went black, and still.

Ginny walked along the warm sands of the shoreline behind the cottage. Close by, her grandmother sat in a deck chair, reading a book about goldfinches; she looked up and waved. Ginny waved back and walked on.

The sand burned, so she stepped into the shallows; her ankles brushed against the turquoise seaweed: '*This all feels so familiar.'*

Ginny looked up, and watched her grandmother carrying the deck chair back home; she tried to call out, but her voice was lost. The sea lapped around her thighs: *'I know what happens next.'* She leapt to run, but the seaweed bound her legs and dragged her under.

She pulled, and tore, and thrashed herself free, and screamed out for her grandmother. Her grandmother turned, and waved goodbye. The seaweed swarmed, and Ginny drowned.

Gasping and weeping, she ripped the wires from her skin.

Dr Turner burst into the room, panic and fury plain on his face. 'What are you doing?' he cried. 'Is everything all right?' He stared at the machines.

'It happened again! You promised to help me! Where were you and what were you doing?'

Dr Turner's anger seeped into his skin. 'I am here to help, but to do that I first need to watch you. It's the beginning of a long journey; I thought you understood.' He glared at Ginny, who nodded in apology.

Dr Turner sat down and rested his hand on her knee. His touch was warm and coarse. 'What happened?'

Ginny recounted her dream: 'I drowned all over again. I remember dying like that before; in a dream, I mean. Not when I was young.'

'Like lucid dreaming?'

Ginny, unsure, shook her head.

He continued: 'Lucid dreaming is when you awaken to the fact that you're dreaming. What you describe sounds similar: a dreaming déjà vu.' He summoned his smile. 'Has this ever happened before?'

'I don't think so; at least, I can't say.'

'No matter; we know it's happened once. It may work as an antidote for your apnea. If you were fluent at lucid dreaming, you might wake before you choke, even avoid it altogether. Imagine guiding your dreams to whatever end you want?'

'I'd like that,' said Ginny.

She continued to attend the clinic.

At home, she kept a dream diary and woke in the night to write notes amidst sleep. She dreaded the loss of any one thought; every dream was precious. They mapped her fears and marked her joys. 'If I remember the trails, I can trace my way to safety.'

But as the nights became easier, each morning, the empty cottage grew larger.

Ginny preferred going home at dusk.

She joined the village craft club to burn away the sunlight.

'What do you want to learn?' asked the secretary. Her face was just like Ginny's, only loveless.

'What classes last the longest?'

'Glass blowing drags on; it starts again next week.'

'I'd like to learn that, please.'

The secretary sighed, and collected the forms.

The teacher's name was Mr Fresnel. He was tall, and grey, and gaunt. His wearied cardigan hung on him like a death shroud, but a boy smiled behind his beard.

The class were few. Mr Fresnel made a baker's dozen. Ginny was the youngest by an age, bar one.

'I'm Phoebe,' said the girl, offering Ginny her hand.

Ginny smiled and clasped the elfin fingers in hers. They were cold, slight, and light like a wraith's; her oak-green eyes smouldered.

'Today, I'd like to teach you the basics of this craft,' began Mr Fresnel. 'And maybe, if we're lucky, a little lore on our hallowed souls. Tonight you'll each take home a handful of Dutchmen's Tears; the pinnacle expression of fragility and strength.'

With the tip of his blowpipe, he scooped a small molten orb of glass from the furnace, and Ginny thought of toast and honey. In a swift arc, he swung the pipe free from the flames and held it over a rain bucket. Fine silken strands broke free and dove into the water, hissing solid as they sank.

Mr Fresnel breathed small puffs of air into the pipe, and a dew of blistering droplets cascaded into the depths. 'It's sublime,' whispered Ginny. The old glassblower peaked his eyebrows and gave a soft bow. When the glass ceased to rain, he reached into the water with paternal care and retrieved a delicate teardrop. 'Everyone take one by the bulb,' he said, displaying his treasure with glee. 'But please, beware of the tail.'

'They look like jewelled tadpoles,' said Ginny.

'A fine description, my dear,' he replied. Ginny blushed. 'Everyone follow me, and carry your amphibians with care.'

The class formed a rudimentary crucible around the refectory table and watched, as he raised a wooden mallet above the glassed ellipse. A mischievous grin stretched his beard, as he let the weight drop down. The jeweled tear glittered.

'What sorcery is this?' laughed Phoebe.

Mr Fresnel conjured his impish grin once more, and nipped the tear's flailing tail. The glass exploded, and the air flashed in a rainbow of dust.

The class was silent.

'There's no magic here but Physics,' said Mr Fresnel, pinching the bulb of a tear and throwing it against the wall; another fleeting rainbow burst. 'You can learn to form so many shapes from glass, but these tears remain unique. They are quite like us, I feel; they are powerful and strong, yet delicate and vulnerable. They seem almost divine.'

One by one, the class took turns blowing tears, until the sun submitted to the moon. Ginny was the last. As she breathed through the blowpipe and watched the scolding shards fall, she felt the same calm she found whilst floating underwater.

'It's so soothing,' she sighed, once the last tear dropped.

'It's your slow breathing,' said Mr Fresnel. 'It's narcotic.'

Ginny was sad it was over so soon.

The class wrapped their best tears in linen rags and bound them as a knapsack.

'Tomorrow, we'll try for a crystal clear bauble,' said the boy in the beard, as he walked his class to the door. 'One moment please, Ginny,' he said, *sotto voce*, as she ambled her way past him. They waited while the others left. 'You show true talent, my girl. There's always one pupil each year that does, and this year I think that's you. Breathing like you did takes time for most folk. I look forward to watching you work.'

Ginny blushed, thanked him, and bounded outside.

Phoebe stood there waiting. 'What did he want?'

'He told me I was good.'

'He's right. Your tears are far more beautiful than mine.'

Ginny's eyes welled: *Is this what a sister feels like?* She smiled. 'You can have one if you want?'

'I couldn't!' whispered Phoebe. 'Could I?'

'I don't mind. Let's swap: one of mine for one of yours.'

'Mine look horrid!' said Phoebe, hiding her linen clutch.

'It's only fair; otherwise, I keep the lot.'

Phoebe's eyes burnished under the moon. 'Thank you, Ginny; you're really very lovely.'

Ginny blushed once more.

The two girls kissed and said goodnight.

Mr Fresnel's inkling came true: Ginny was blessed with a natural talent. Her fledgling skill found complex form, as blossom reveals its fruit.

'I'm forever here,' was always her answer, whenever the curious begged for her secret.

'She's an artist!' exclaimed Mr Fresnel, blatant with pride. 'Addicted to chasing perfection for life. She'll only quit when she's dead.'

Ginny allowed him his fantasy, but her craft was never more than a distraction. She chased perfection as a known delusion, but still her chore was infinite.

Each hour cast in the furnace was sacrificed to hasten the sunrise, when her grandmother was sure to wake. Each morning was a promise broken; her penance deemed unworthy.

'Her sleep remains peaceful,' explained Dr Turner. 'No one has witnessed a moment's twitch of fear. More patience is all I advise.' Such were the words reeled off in rote whenever Ginny asked, and always the question invoked and followed: 'But how are you, and your dreams?'

Ginny was vexed to confess that, unlike her grandmother, she was healing. 'My diary is an atlas of fading ill thoughts. I reread it to remember, and so in sleep recall the uncanny. As the pages fill, the presence of the nightmares wanes. They feel familiar, but also benign, and seem to seed content instead. I wander, uncurious, and know I'm only sleeping.'

Dr Turner donned his smile. 'Your sleep does seem more stable; you seldom wake up breathless. What about attacks at home? Are they as rare as here?'

'Yes, but I still avoid sleep, if I can. I rest better exhausted.'

Dr Turner shook his head. 'Clockwork circadian rhythm is essential. Enduring fatigue to ensure you sleep is unwise for the mind, and unhealthy for the body. You've learned to shape your dreams; what do you want to avoid?'

'I'm not adept yet, like you want.'

'Experience will cure you, I promise.'

Ginny sighed. 'Sometimes only my eyes wake. I look around my room, but my body refuses to follow.'

'Somnolent paralysis,' the doctor whispered, his sibilance

hissed with a grimace. 'The body remains in unconscious stasis, while the mind flees from Morpheus. Folklorists would have you believe that it's daemons or djinn that jinx us with a whim to possess the soul; but that's moonshine and hogwash, of course.

Ginny was not so certain. 'Sometimes I see someone standing by my bed: a silhouette, or shadow, like a ghost.'

'Ephemeral spectrum bleeding from your dreams; nothing more, nothing less; nothing else.'

Ginny was unconvinced.

That night, at the clinic, the veiled wraith returned.

Her eyelids parted to the soothing glow of the nautilus shell. The blackened sky was cloudless and punctured with scattered starlight. Her heart sank, while she lay static, suppressed under an arc of gravity. It bored though her breast, while the wraith lingered by the door, and watched.

But Ginny was more curious of the second lurking shadow. In the far-right corner, his face guised in the gloaming, sat the undeniable mass of Dr Turner.

Ginny stared out from her skeletal cell to the blackened recess, where she was certain his coarse glare burrowed into her.

He rose and walked towards the bed, oblivious to the silent silhouette that trailed behind him.

The nautilus shell twitched in the moonlight. The whole room froze. A dreadful minute passed.

Dr Turner crept one cautious step, and the nautilus shell crashed to the floor. Ginny bolted awake and the wraith collapsed.

'Are you all right?' whispered Dr Turner, his bulk still as bronze, his skin cast stiff and waxen.

'Why are you here?'

The doctor stared at the nautilus shards. 'I thought I ought to wait and watch, perchance of witnessing your night terrors.'

'Did you?'

He glanced at Ginny, but faltered under her gaze. 'I'm uncertain. I'm afraid.'

'What about the shadow by the door?'

Dr Turner hesitated, and gathered the nautilus fragments from the floor. 'Nothing happened here that I can't explain; do you understand? Imagination is dangerous.'

Ginny nodded.

The doctor left.

The wraith continued to watch Ginny sleeping. It came and left the cottage as a sparrow does a garden, and Ginny began to long for it when she woke and it was absent.

The clinic, however, was another matter; there, she was forever certain to see its silken form cascade the empty corner.

Dr Turner maintained his ignorance of its presence, and never returned to check.

Phoebe was more sympathetic. 'There's more magic in this world, and in Heaven, than in any whimsy we dream,' she said, one night, as she walked home from the glasswork studio with Ginny. She smiled, and linked her arm in Phoebe's. Phoebe clasped her hand. 'There are other ways of finding sleep, you know; exhaustion is a little dull.'

'Well, how else, darling nurse?'

Phoebe's sly lips spread. 'Take me home, and I'll show you.'

At the cottage, under candlelight, by the crackling, kindled hearth, Phoebe pressed a small glass phial into Ginny's cool palm. 'Drink it down and lie with me, and I'll drink one as well.'

'What's this?'

'Magic.'

'A potion?'
'A tincture.'
'Of what?
'Love.'
Ginny watched the firelight flicker across the emerald elixir. 'What will it do?'
'The flowers draw away the world, until all that's left is you and I, and we alone; as love will.'
'I simply drink, and wait?'
'We drink, then lie, and wait as one.'
In bed, imbibed, entwined, they dreamt.
Ginny was the smaller spoon; Phoebe's hand lay still by her lips, still glistening from a lingering kiss, the ebb and flow of their bosoms harmonious.
Ginny was a swaddled child.
Hazel eyes smiled; cherry lips loved; auburn curls fell.
This was once her mother.
She blinked, and warm tears cleansed her face.
Golden light confessed its love.
Ginny was a delicate girl.
Her grandmother's hands clasped over her own and guided her fingers to weave yellow wool. 'Knitting's a knack that takes time, my darling; have patience, sweet Gin, have patience.'
Teardrops gleamed under amorous gold.
Ginny was a little madam. There's more to life than books and birds!' she cried from the garden shadows.
The swallows fled, and the starlings followed, and her grandmother looked up and smiled. 'Perhaps,' she replied, and read on.
Gilt-leaf fell on her saline skin.
Ginny was a young woman.
'Wake up. Wake up,' she begged, clutching her grandmother's hand. But the words were as silence, and Ginny a wraith in the presence of a slumbering corpse.

The halcyon radiance instilled valediction and Ginny, awakening, wept. 'I need more time,' she choked.

Phoebe stirred and nuzzled into Ginny, murmuring notes of a lullaby. 'Good morning, dreamer.' A slow kiss caressed Ginny's neck. 'Where did she take you?'

'Who?'

'The emerald ghost.'

'Oh. Somewhere beautiful, and honest.'

'I promise she loves you; I'm sure she loves me.'

'Where did she take you?'

'Somewhere wonderful.'

'Did you cry?'

'Always.'

'Are you sad?'

'Not now.'

'But asleep?'

Phoebe sighed. 'It's disillusion; I listen, enlighten, and learn.'

'What if I'm too late?'

'No one who asks ever is.'

But Phoebe had misunderstood.

'Is she still peaceful?' asked Ginny, as she stroked her grandmother's arm. The skin on the bone was loose and thin.

'She's shown no signs of waking,' Dr Turner duly explained, 'and last night, for a moment, her heart stopped.'

Ginny's pulse grew violent. 'Will she ever wake?'

He led Ginny from the ward. 'As long as she lives, she still has a chance, but the chance that she has is slim.'

'I won't give up on her.'

'Then don't. She never gave up on you.'

Ginny nodded and smiled.

'Good girl.' He grinned. 'Now let's get you to sleep.'

The hospital bed, though firm and thin, had become

familiar and welcome. Ginny felt the room was hers. She greeted the clock in her customary salute: 'Still spinning, I see. That's good; me too.'

She missed the broken nautilus shell, and so brought her own from home. She placed it on the windowsill, and watched the moonlight shimmer on its amber surface.

'Where did you find that?' Dr Turner demanded.

'My mantelpiece; it's mine.'

'Will you take it away tomorrow?'

'Yes.'

'Good.'

The doctor left, and Ginny soon slept.

She awoke, in soul alone, paralysed in the dawning twilight.

The wraith lingered by the door, but Ginny paid it no mind. Her thoughts were on the nautilus shell. She gazed along its spiral form and followed its unseen infinity.

The shell began to rock.

If only you were bigger, she thought, *you might roll right over the sill.*

The swaying shell climbed its arc.

Can you hear me?

The spiral flipped, and landed on its blunted limit.

Ginny bolted awake, and the wraith collapsed. The shell was still, sitting steady on its end. She lay back and smiled.

'I want us to lie like before,' said Ginny. She glanced around the studio, but no one seemed to notice.

Phoebe feigned a coquette's smile. 'What do you mean?'

Ginny blushed, and burned. 'Please, don't tease,' she begged in whisper, 'I know you know what I say; let's drink your elixir again.'

Phoebe leaned forward and whispered with a pout, 'I've been counting the days 'til you asked.'

Ginny glowed. 'So, when? How soon?'

'Tonight after class?'

'Yes.'

Phoebe's eyes shone. 'I always carry two, just in case.'

'Carry two of what, and for whom?' asked Mr Fresnel. He appeared from behind, as a silent apparition

'Nothing,' said Phoebe. 'Only girlish trinkets.'

Ginny's heart surged.

Mr Fresnel raised an eyebrow, but asked her nothing more. He smiled at Ginny and looked at her workbench. 'And what will you dazzle me with this week?

'A twelve-hour sandglass, I hope.'

'Ah, to follow the dying day?'

'To fall throughout the night: a gift for my grandmother. It'll be the first thing she sees when she wakes.'

Mr Fresnel's gaze welled. 'Let's fill it with spectacular glass.'

He led her to the cellar. The stale air was fragrant with the taste of the sea. Dozens of sand-sacks lay strewn around the room in thick, lazy mounds, and the walls were lined from floor to roof with wide oak shelves, each one home to a myriad of jars, filled with twinkling dust: a jewelled apothecary of glass.

'Pick any colour you like.'

For Ginny, there was only one choice. 'The dark green.'

'A fine selection: olivine quartz, born of volcano; a tempestuous crystal, like our teardrops. Your sandglass will be a thing of beauty.'

He handed her the jar, and the contents flickered in the gaslight, as dying embers in a hearth.

She followed him upstairs.

On the threshold, he hesitated. 'I see you and Phoebe have grown fond of each other.'

Ginny's heart stilled.

Mr Fresnel turned, and continued. 'I'm happy for you,

Ginny. If it's love, it's a rare treasure.'

Ginny stayed silent but smiled.

'Be careful of where love leads you, though. Phoebe will mean well, but folly is so simple in youth. It's far easier to fall when you're dizzy. Remember, nothing lasts, yet nothing is lost.'

'Are you sure?' asked Phoebe.

Ginny nodded. 'I love you.'

They poured the elixir, swallowed its sweetness, and kissed. Imbibed, in bliss, their bodies wove, and lay as one. Ginny ascended to aurulent luminescence. She had been here before, and had bathed in its tears.

'Where am I?' she whispered.

No answer echoed, but she felt she was safe.

'*Why am I here?*

The flaxen world blazed and blinded her; she was loved.

'*Who are you?*

Honeyed teardrops whet her soul. Ginny smiled and wept. Ascending, she listened, enlightened.

'*May I stay?*

The silken folds of seraphic flames fused and wreathed around her. Revelation in immolation.

All went quiet and still. All was cold and black.

Ginny woke to a somnolent Phoebe. She kissed her elfin fingers and purred a hushed lullaby.

Pallid dawn loomed.

Ginny set her sandglass beside her grandmother's bed, and the gleaming olivine fragments began their slow descent. 'Goodnight,' she said, and kissed her withered lips.

'No news of recovery to report, I'm afraid,' stated Dr Turner.

'I'll see her soon, I'm sure,' replied Ginny.

Dr Turner grimaced. 'Tomorrow's another day.'

He led her to the clinic in silence.

Alone, she placed her nautilus shell back on the moonlit sill, and stood it on its spiral limit. It sat quite still and glimmered. She watched its lunar rainbow nimbus radiate around its golden arc, until her mind's eye opened and she slept.

Amidst unwelcome dreams, she awoke again in paralysis.

In the corner, the wraith watched; but Ginny was oblivious, the nautilus shell entrancing her. It twitched forward: once, twice, thrice, then toppled, and landed on its helical edge.

Ginny smiled inside and her will held.

The shell turned a slow circle, heavy in her head. It rotated like a minute hand meandering a watch, as its corkscrew crept ever closer to the edge. The weight pushed back, like a stubborn clock-key.

At the brink of the sill, she held the shell still, until her will yielded to inertia. The nautilus fell and shattered.

When Ginny woke to its piercing scream, the wraith was already gone. She smiled, and daydreamed through 'til dawn.

'Did you bring two phials for tonight?' whispered Ginny.

The faux-coy Phoebe whispered, 'Yes.'

In the cottage, under candles, near the hearthside, close as skin, they drank the emerald liquor.

In poisoned bliss, their bodies braided. Ginny soared to celestial ochroid. She felt she was home.

Hello? Salus? I'm here, she thought.

The rapturous saffron lustre swirled, and revealed a sparkling pearl. It winked, and swelled, then washed away, and Ginny was tranquil in solace.

She drifted on waves, uncurious; content to be loved. Silent, until the iridescence died.

All was black and cold; all went still and quiet.

She woke to Phoebe's gentle aria, her Sapphic voice divine. Ginny pulled her slender frame in line along her own. 'Good morning, dreamer,' she whispered.

Phoebe's song lulled her to rest. She rolled around and bound her limbs to Ginny. 'Good morning, lover.'

But the morning was already over; the sun hung high overhead.

'I'm sorry I broke your beautiful shell,' said Ginny.

Her grandmother was unresponsive.

'I'll find you another. I promise.' She kissed the dry furrows of her forehead. 'Goodnight.' She reset the sandglass.

There was no need to ask about her grandmother's condition; Dr Turner's ambivalence told her everything. She made her own way to the clinic.

The bare windowsill was dull and flat; the moon was new and veiled. Ginny turned away to ignore the guilt the glaring void made plain.

She stared at the clock and watched the golden second hand revolve an endless hour.

Numbed by its steadfast rhythm, lethargy soon enveloped her vision and seduced her mind to sleep. But her unconscious soul was restless.

Eclipsed in subliminal caliginosity, Ginny lay petrified.

The wraith observed, impassive.

Ginny's gaze locked on the clock, and followed the meridian minute. She fixed her sight on the second-hand tip, as it tripped around the perimeter. When it passed "IX", she willed it still. The golden tick-tock stopped.

She clung and hung like a spectral plumb-line, clockwork and synapse in stalemate.

Her eyes closed; her breath held. She pulled. The cogs crunched, yielded and started to rewind; torsion buckled in surrender, and the past hour fast unwound.

Exhausted and breathless, Ginny choked herself

conscious. The wraith collapsed. The slow clock clicked forward, its resolute gears now late.

Dr Turner burst into the room. 'Are you all right?'

'Yes,' said Ginny, with mocking gratitude.

The doctor nodded. He glanced at his watch and recorded the time. '2.17am,' he muttered.

'Is it not only one?' asked Ginny, with secret glee.

He stared at the clock. 'Ignore it. It's slow.' Then he left.

Ginny was enthralled by her nocturnal magic. *All I require is patience and practice*, she thought. *And, of course, more emerald elixir*. She lay restless, lost in mantra, and drifted on desire 'til sunrise.

'Can we lie again tonight?' asked Ginny.

'Whenever you wish, my love,' said Phoebe.

Under starlight, in the cottage, in a ritual now instinctual, the two girls kissed and lay as warp and weft; a knot of toxic rapture.

Ginny transcended the carnal, to Heaven, suspended in caramel candescence.

'*Salus*,' she breathed, and the *lumus*, in love, engulfed her.

All was white and still.

Ginny woke in trembling arms, as teardrops fell to her face. 'I thought I'd lost you,' cried Phoebe. 'I thought you'd never wake.'

'What happened?' The cottage was in dusk.

'You slept all day, and breathed so slowly,' wept Phoebe. 'Please tell me, where did you go?'

'Nowhere,' whispered Ginny.

Phoebe collapsed in hysterics; tears cascaded her body.

'Never mind,' Ginny murmured. 'I'm safe.'

'There were complications last night,' said Dr Turner. 'Mrs Greenwood suffered a heart attack. Her chances of waking are nil.'

Ginny's stomach flooded cold. 'Why?'

'Her brain shows no signs of life.'

'What else can we do?' she pleaded.

'Nothing. I need your permission to extinguish her life.'

'I'm not ready.'

'*She* is.'

'Can it wait until morning?'

'If it must,' sighed the doctor.

'I want to say goodnight, one last time.'

Ginny held her grandmother's hand and whispered Phoebe's lullaby. She turned the olivine sandglass with teardrops on her cheeks. 'Goodnight. I love you. Goodnight.'

In her bed in the clinic, dulled by morphine, Ginny seeped tears, until she drifted into nightmare. She fought its clutch, and opened her eyes to the faint silhouette of the wraith.

Static, and incensed, she vowed to wreck the mocking clock. When the golden hand clicked "IX", breath held, she pulled.

Time stopped.

She smiled.

With eyes closed, she spun the minutes backwards, until her aching lungs heaved. Her gasping body bolted forward and she saw the wraith was gone.

Ginny stared at the clock face; it had rewound three hours.

Dr Turner entered. 'What happened?'

'A nightmare; I'm sorry, I feel quite disturbed.'

He nodded. 'I'll give you another dose in two hours.'

'Is the clock still slow?' smiled Ginny.

The doctor checked his watch. 'Not now; it's exact.'

He left, and Ginny waited, while the minutes passed 'til dawn.

Before the morning died, Ginny watched her grandmother give up the ghost.

'It's for the best, my darling,' said the nurse. Ginny, though broken, agreed. She placed the olivine sandglass in her bag and left.

'Are you all right?' asked Mr Fresnel. Ginny was lost to the furnace, in hypnosis.

'I will be,' she whispered. 'I only wish we'd had more time. I want her to know that I love her.'

'She does, I'm sure; don't doubt it.'

'She showed me time is precious, but I can never thank her.'

The boy in Mr Fresnel smiled. 'Life rarely follows a straight and simple course, Ginny; more often it meanders in spirals. We revisit truths we thought we once knew, and find that we missed their meaning. We're destined to redefine our convictions. One day your guilt will pass, and will so without shame. The love and thanks are often unsaid, but never unfelt: nothing lasts, yet nothing is lost.' He squeezed her shoulder, and resumed his encouraging patrol of his studio

Ginny took Phoebe's hand. 'Will you stay with me tonight, please? Only you, no elixir.'

'Until the sunrise finds us,' whispered Phoebe, and sealed her promise with a kiss.

The cottage was lit by firelight. Phoebe slept on Ginny's breast. Her soft auburn hair was sweet and soothing, but still Ginny lay pensive.

With slow, maternal delicacy, Ginny placed Phoebe's head on a pillow. 'Sweet dreams, my love.' She crept from the room, and returned with the olivine sandglass.

The hearth smouldered with ash and ember. Ginny fed kindling to its heat, and phoenix fire blazed. She closed her eyes and sealed the flue. 'I'm so sorry,' she whispered.

On the mantelpiece, where the nautilus shell once rocked, Ginny set the sandglass to watch the olivine cascade. She sat before the choking fire as a lotus, and clasped Phoebe's hand; she stirred, but Ginny murmured lullaby and stilled her.

Plumes of black smoke filled the cottage. Ginny focused on the falling grains of emerald glass. Breath held, she pushed; time wound down and ceased. With eyes closed, she waited and bore the heaving weight. The black smoke that caressed her skin hung as static fog. Her heart slowed, still as a rock, and her lungs seared and locked, but the olivine glass still failed to fall.

All went cold and quiet; all was black, and still.

Ginny's lungs filled with the scent of lemon soap.

'Is that you?' asked Ginny.

Golden flames engulfed the darkness, and love's undying light consumed her.

'*I knew I'd find you,*' she said, in her head.

'*We never leave; we always watch.*'

'*May I stay?*'

Only silence answered, as crystalline teardrops exploded in the burning ether.

Below, the lustrous flutes of empyreal flame swelled and weaved a wreath. Molten cords of seething light bound to Ginny's legs and dragged her under; a pearl orb glimmered, and winked.

All was black.

All was null.

THE SESSION

By Nina Oram

December 23rd: the Winter Solstice and the original first day of the season. It was just past two and already the town lay half in darkness. The rainclouds that had blown in off the Atlantic had got no further – too low maybe – and, like thunder, got stuck between the town's steep sides. They rolled around the valley, bouncing from one side to the other, dropping water in the way a Christmas tree being dragged out of the house in the New Year drops needles.

I left the river, the old stone bridge, and walked uphill, past a line of shops. They were packed, thick with the warm, damp bodies of people who had been waiting so long for a break in the rain that they'd given up the pretence of browsing and were now *actually* browsing. I passed the misted windows, stepped through the stream that ran the length of the pavement. Felt it splash the bottom of my trousers, pierce the seam of my right shoe and wet my sock, my big toe, and sighed with distaste. It was too cold, too wet. It was always the same here, on the edge of Ireland's west, the northern gateway to Connemara.

I gave up and made my way back to the hotel, turning left at the clock tower. The mountain behind it, rising up first high and then long, with its pilgrim path (millennia upon millennia of worn white against the brown), was obscured by the cloud, its shadow just another grey in a sky full of greys; shades of winter white.

I pushed through the revolving door and entered the hotel foyer. Saw the receptionist lift her head over the top of

164

the desk and give me a friendly smile. It was too late in the year, too out of season for a lone tourist to be inconspicuous, so reluctantly I flashed her my brightest smile back. The wide one, full of teeth.

I'm a merger. I prefer the anonymity of the crowd, the darkness of the shadows, a glimpse out of the corner of the eye. But it costs nothing to be friendly and, sometimes, if you get the right person, you get something back and a little more besides.

I went upstairs. My room, the only one occupied on the fourth and highest floor, looked out onto the street. It was too hot. The heat of the room blasted me as I opened the door and stepped inside. I moved to the windows, opened the one nearest the bed and then, slipping off my shoes and coat, lay down. In the gloom, the sound of the cars in the rain, the tyres turning, splashing through the wet, soothed me and I slept.

When I woke, it was dark. The rain had long gone, but the streets below me glistened and the air through my bedroom window smelt fresh, sweet. I felt better, rested. Even though I hadn't eaten I had no need for food. It was time to go, my instincts told me so; my instincts, and that tiny, familiar thrill of anticipation I allowed myself.

Slipping my feet into my shoes, I moved over to the dressing table. My case, the one I'd had made especially for my instrument, was waiting there for me. Long and thin, it was crafted from resin the colour of amber, fire. To the unknowing it looked solid enough, seemed without join or seam, but was in fact two parts carefully cut, shaped so as to slip smoothly together and apart. Hiding, or revealing, the instrument within with a simple twist of the hand. The design, devilishly clever, was my own. A one off, unique. I picked it up, let my fingers run along its length, before allowing it to settle neatly into my palm.

The man who made it for me had such talent. A master of

his craft. The best money could buy. The accident was such a shame, such a waste.

I sighed sadly, regretfully. Wished things could've been different.

My coat was still a little damp, the material catching as I placed a reluctant arm into each sleeve. Then I left my room, closing the door firmly behind me, only letting go of the handle when I heard the lock click. The corridor was empty; there was no one to see me as I moved swiftly, silently – windowless, narrow walls on either side – down the stairs. In the foyer, the earlier receptionist was gone and a new one was sitting there. Younger, prettier and more careless. She was too engrossed in the magazine she kept hidden across her knees to look up. Piqued by her attitude, her indifference to me, I made a mental note.

Outside, I walked back the way I'd come earlier, past the clock tower and down the hill. The night air was sharp, bitter. While I'd slept, the weather had turned even colder, the wind changing direction, blowing now down from the Arctic, its icy bite chilling my face and hands. The street was quiet, everyone safely, sensibly, indoors. I passed a pub, heard music, the people inside talking and laughing through the closed door. I continued on, passed another one; a third, a fourth, but still I didn't stop. There was only one I wanted: McGourty's; on the corner, with dusty bottles in the window and one woodworm-scarred wooden crate. A traditional pub, revamped, made to look old for the tourists. I reached it, pushed the door open, and stepped inside.

The place was packed, filled mainly with tourists jostling for space and the last vacant seat, and a few local farmers clinging desperately to their usual stools at the bar. Where they'd all come from, I had no idea. In the dark and the cold, the streets, the town, had seemed half dead, lifeless. But I knew why they'd come.

For the music: that's why everyone comes. Even me.

I scanned the room, plotting my route, then began to squeeze my way through the bodies. Breathed a silent curse as I nudged a couple reluctant to move not so gently to one side. Behind the bar a good looking young man was serving, pouring two glasses of Guinness, the landlord watching him from his stool placed to one side. I saw the look on his face, the ambivalence, in one moment of bittersweet irony. To have a place packed to the rafters with people, with not an inch of space left, not even for standing; and yet, mostly they were couples, walkers in matching rainproof jackets, sensible shoes, and students from Southern Europe – half a pint, a glass, lasting them most of the night.

Not a lot of profit in that. Not enough to make Pat McGourty's pumps fly, to make his greedy little heart and his tills sing.

Drink in hand, I headed for the back of the pub. Realised that they'd changed more than just the outside since my last visit. What used to be the hall, the side entrance into the lounge, the old, ladies bar, was now an oddly shaped, drafty little room with stools along one wall and a rough plank of wood fixed above them to rest a pint on. It was a cold place, lacking in atmosphere, and yet it too was packed. More squeezing and I was through and into the back. The session was in full swing. It wasn't a large one, but the room was small and, with all the cases and other musical accoutrements, there was little room left for the listeners and the drinkers to sit in. Not that it looked like anyone minded having to stand. These players were the real thing: aged, grey to silver to white (though no one would ever think it from the speed of their fingers, their breath). From the Gaeltacht. They finished their song and the crowd clapped. Their leader, the fiddler player, nodded his head and smiled, gracious; but the others, taking the applause as their due, ignored it and took a long eager sup of their drinks instead.

A few moments, a few more sups later, and the fiddler nodded again, this time to the man with the bodhran. He grinned in reply and lifted his drum, his right hand poised and then, with a tap of his foot, he began. The sound was soft, warm, the beat of a heart, unstoppable as the man's hand flew back and forth, back and forth. In front of him, the crowd fell silent. No one coughed, shifted their feet or moved, not even to lift a drink. Even at the front bar, people quietened. I could almost see the looks, the nudges. Shhh, shhh, listen, listen, *listen*. Without a sound, the other musicians lifted their instruments, settled their feet, hands, fingers and mouths, and waited. Waited, poised for that one perfect moment. A few more beats of a heart, a few more seconds of held breath, and they began. They hit it, and even those who didn't know the music heard it and knew, sensed that they were listening to something special. I moved towards the front, swaying with the bodies around me, then side stepping, slipping into the gaps they left. Found one tall stool left unnoticed in the corner, under the window.

This time, as the music finished, the crowd whooped and yelled along with their clapping, and the fiddler pressed the bodhran player's shoulder, urging him to his feet to take one awkward, embarrassed bow. The rest took another drink; one or two, I noticed, looked my way. I saw the accordion player nudge the leader and, not wanting to seem too keen, I glanced away, seemingly indifferent. Looked casually back and saw that the leader too was staring at me, his gaze taking in the case lying across my knees, kept in place by one hand.

'Ya play?' he asked, raising his voice slightly.

'Yes.' I nodded.

'Any good?'

'Not bad.'

He studied me for a moment longer, as if trying to make up his mind.

'We're down a man,' he said eventually, his only explanation as he threw out a foot, caught one of the crossbars of the stool sat under the table, and pushed it out towards me.

I stood up, aware of the stares of the people around me, and joined the group. No one said anything; just watched as I twisted the case and slipped the top off. The low whistle gleamed a steely grey in the light of the fire as I took it out, felt the metal cold between my fingers, across my palm.

'Do ya want to warm it?'

I shook my head.

He frowned, but made no comment.

'Do ya know "Sally Gardens"?' he asked then.

I nodded again and, lifting the whistle to my lips, placed each finger – behind the knuckle, not the tip – over the holes.

'You go first, and we'll follow.'

I took a deep breath and began. A few in the crowd had turned away, regulars maybe, sceptical of an interloper, a pretender; but as I played the first few notes, they turned quickly back.

If you've never heard the low whistle, let me describe it for you: it's a paradox, a modern invention that sounds old, ancient. Gets hold of your guts and pulls them up through you, into your heart and throat, then up, towards the heavens. Floating and soaring like the flute; deep and resonant like the oboe, yet strangely earthy, as if it's been carved, moulded from wood, bamboo or clay, instead of cold, smooth metal. Beautiful, haunting, irresistible. If they were truly as old as they sounded, then Pan would surely have had one.

The musicians were looking at one another. I nodded once, my head bobbing up and down, the low whistle going with me, and they caught my meaning straight away. They joined me, following my lead effortlessly, each instrument – the fiddle, bodhran, mandolin, tin whistle and accordion – finding the gaps left by my low whistle and making them their own. The notes twisted and turned; the music swelled, threatened to burst, and I marvelled at how good the band were. They were the best I'd found for a very long time. The last verse. I let my low whistle linger at the very end. Then the song finished and the listeners went wild.

Pat McGourty appeared suddenly, parting the cheering crowd, the young barman behind him carrying a tray heavy, dipping with the weight of pints crammed on top of it.

'Seamus, that was fecking brilliant,' Pat said as he joined us, grinning from ear to ear. 'I swear they heard that in Tommy Murphy's bar.'

Tommy Murphy, I knew, was his deadliest rival, his closest competitor. The fiddler, Seamus, nodded, and tried to look nonchalant, but I sensed his heart swell.

'Here, have another drink, lads. On the house.'

The musicians quickly finished their drinks, and stacked the glasses as the young barman began to refill the table, balancing the tray carefully as he emptied it.

'And there's one for you,' Pat said suddenly, turning to look at me.

'I'm grand.' I nodded to my pint, which was two-thirds full.

'I'll have it,' the bodhran player interjected quickly, leaning over and closing his fingers around the top before anyone else could.

The young barman squeezed past the musicians and went over to the fire, gave it a poke, stoking it up before adding more logs and turf.

'It's on the house.' Pat was insistent.

'I don't like to drink too much,' I replied, seeing the young barman's face turn downwards, and remembering the look of the young receptionist from the hotel. 'It interferes with my playing.'

'I've no such bother.' The bodhran player laughed, his Guinness-shaped belly jiggling. He placed the pint carefully, lovingly, next to his own.

Pat McGourty was frowning at me, conscious that I was

refusing his hospitality, and drawing unwanted attention to myself. I backtracked. 'Maybe there's no harm, just this once.'

The bodhran player's glass froze on its way to his mouth and he gave me a look of dismay.

'You keep that one; I'll get him another,' MacGourty said loudly, both eyes sliding sideways and snatching a look at the audience. Making sure they knew of his benevolence, his generosity, and hoping it might encourage them to drink up and have another themselves.

The clock on the mantelpiece said half ten as he turned away, began moving through the bodies, the young barman with him. They disappeared, the gap behind them closing as the arms and legs reclaimed their spaces. Seamus picked up his fiddle and the rest of the group followed. The mandolin player had lost his mandolin, so was cradling a bouzouki instead.

'"She Moved Through the Fair,"' Seamus murmured to me. 'They'll love it.'

And they did, just as they loved "Rolling in the Rye Grass", and "Mna Na Heireann". Another break, another sup, but this time the crowd were too impatient, too eager to wait. A few called out, encouraging, making requests and Seamus, his face flushed with pleasure and pride, couldn't help but respond. He was on his feet in a heartbeat, his fiddle under his chin, his bow lifted. A few beats of "Drowsy Maggie" and he was pulling us with him, the crowd following fast. We'd barely finished when he waved his hand again and now it was the accordion player's turn. He led us into 'The Blackbird' and out again, and this time there was no break, no stopping, and not even the bodhran player cared.

On and on we played: "Wandering Minstrel", "High Road to Sligo", jig after jig after jig, the tempo slowly building. Seamus was looking at me now, his forehead creasing again, frowning. He knew his music, his instruments, and was wondering at the impossibility of my endless breath. But still he didn't stop, and neither did we. The crowd was tens of people thick now, their heads filling the space all the way to the door and beyond. Watching them, I could see their feet, legs and arms straining; could see how desperately their bodies wanted to move, to dance, to fly.

Just like in the old days.

Half past eleven and Seamus' white hair was lifting and falling, the bodhran player's hand was a blur, and the tin whistle player was almost out of breath. They were getting tired; I knew it, sensed it, just as I knew that the body is weak and the older body weaker still. The musicians slowed, nearing the end of their last reel, and I knew it was time. I stood up, and began to play the first notes of my tune, just as the musicians ended theirs. Tired and weary as they were, they had no thought but to join me, too intoxicated with my music to stop; my whistle urged their flagging spirits on.

Eleven fifty five and it was hard not dance, to caper with the fire, the anticipation that was flowing through me. Midnight was so very close and the low whistle between my fingers was getting hot, scalding, like a poker left too long in the flame. Relentless, it pulled the tempo and the music on, playing faster and faster and dragging the musicians after. I watched them as their fingers, hands, feet and lips flew. Watched their bodies of skin, hair and sweat breathe as one, in perfect rhythm with each other and the music, and knew in that one moment they were more alive than they'd ever been. Seamus was looking at me again, his eyes widening as he finally realised who I was, even as his fingers kept moving and his arm kept pumping. The oldest there, born of another generation and another time, he knew me from the old stories: the pacts made at the crossroads, the legends of Midsummer nights and stone circles. He knew they had to stop before the end of the day. But it was too late. Like a falling body caught by the pull of gravity, so my low whistle pulled him inexorably on. The crowd behind me were listening with eyes half closed, mesmerised, their feet moving by themselves, but I ignored them.

It was the musicians I wanted: their music.

The clock's hand touched twelve. I heard the first chime and, for a moment, winter and night kept the turn towards spring and sunlight at bay. And then I was lifting my head, my low whistle soaring, the notes impossibly loud, and the fire in the grate flared. Too high, it licked the top of the mantelpiece, the sides of the wall, spilled out into the room. The musicians froze, half turned and, framed by the flames, I saw them as they were soon going to be: skin charred and shrivelled to black; empty but for the odd, singed hair and edges of bone, splitting through soft roasted flesh, protruding outwards.

I slowed, let my music fade and, for those that listened, the perfection of it was gone too soon, too quickly to savour or remember. I smiled to myself, knowing that without their remembering, this moment would be forever looked for, dreamt of and missed. And then the crowd saw the flames, realised what it meant, and the screaming began.

The night air was cold as I stepped outside, the street eerily quiet against the screams and shouts behind me, and the roar and whoosh of the fire as it took hold. I walked uphill, heard the pub door open and everything grew suddenly louder, as people staggered out, coughing, choking, crying. Heard a siren wail, then another, and more people began to appear, from the flats over the shops opposite, and the houses over way. Some were worried for their own safety, but most were spectators, drawn irresistibly to the horror. I continued on, back towards my hotel. My low whistle was still warm. I could feel it through the case, the resin made of flesh and bone, keeping it, keeping their music carefully contained.

At the top of the hill, I spotted a young woman stood

beneath the clock tower. She was staring down the hill, caught in the moment by the sight of the inferno, while walking home. She saw me, didn't recognise me, even though I knew her all too well. But at the sight of me, the paralysis left her. With a cry, she was moving, crossing the road, passing me and heading down the hill. I watched the young hotel receptionist go, her feet tripping as she broke out into a run. As she thought of her brother and realised.

The next morning was bright, the sun shining, the sky blue and the air warm, mild. A tacit promise, as enticing as it was false, of an end to the darkness and winter. I left my room, carrying my music case. The hotel was quiet. Those that were inside spoke in hushed, respectful tones. Newspapers had been left on the table next to the hotel entrance, and I paused on my way out long enough to pick one up, and read the front page: six dead – five musicians and a barman. A tragedy. A freak repeat of a fire that had ravaged the very same pub over sixty years ago. Unbelievable, and yet it could have been so much worse, the journalist said, torn between the capriciousness of fate and God's miracle that no more were hurt. I let the paper drop back onto the table; felt my smile twist.

God and Fate had nothing to do with it. People see only what they want to see.

I stepped through the door and, catching the fading scent of smoke, of burning, breathed deeply. One more breath and then I was moving, crossing the road and turning left, up the hill, following the path out of town.

PET

By Valentine Williams

I discovered it one day in the airing cupboard, asleep on a pile of towels. I certainly hadn't gone looking for it, even though the night noises told me it was in the house.

There had also been a strong, unpleasant smell in the place for several days before that, with more than a whiff of rotten fish about it.

As I opened the door, the smell, with its sharp ammonia tang, hit me and my eyes watered. I was surprised that the creature didn't wake. I watched it for a moment and then closed the cupboard door as softly as I could, in order not to disturb it, and went off to do other things. When I next looked into the cupboard it had gone, so I removed the towels and put them into the washing machine to soak.

I returned to the kitchen thinking that, if it had been wandering around the house, it would be hungry. I put out a dish of cat food, left over from when my dear Rummage was alive, not knowing really what else to give it, and listened for its movements that night. But all was silent. The terrible smell had spread throughout my house, but for a while I didn't know where the creature had hidden itself. Finally, I found it again; or rather, it found me.

I was standing by the sink in the kitchen, wondering what I should do, when I heard a tiny noise behind me. I turned slowly, so as not to startle it, and looked down. Under the darkness of the cooker, two tiny red eyes shone out at me. I jumped back in surprise. It was staring at me and did not seem at all inclined to run away. As I bent down to look at it, it came forward towards my feet and offered me its head to stroke. I was nervous, I admit, so I petted it carefully with one finger, mindful of the sharp white teeth poking out from the soft, wet corners of its mouth. It seemed satisfied for the moment and disappeared into a corner of the living room, where I could hear it ripping up paper.

Wiping my hands, I moved into the living room and sat down on the sofa, where I eventually fell asleep. When I woke, it was curled up next to me, if you please. It smelled worse than ever, as if it had been eating the most disgusting sort of garbage. Later, it returned to ripping up paper in the corner again. It slunk out of the living room while I was taking the soiled covers off the cushions, and for a while I didn't know what had happened to it. I think I wished at that point it would just go, and I even left the front door open for a while, hoping it would move on. It didn't.

A day or two later, when I looked in the airing cupboard, it had returned there, making a mess of my clean linen. It snarled at me this time. I shut the door hastily, and left it in peace. Later, it crept out and approached me, gazing at me with a look that was both imploring and menacing. Was it hungry? I never saw it eating, but as the food I left for it disappeared, it must have been eaten when I was not around. It left a disgusting mess in my kitchen, smearing the cat-food all over the floor. And its toilet habits ... the less said about those, the better! But, by this time, it had begun to creep up to me whenever I sat down, and nuzzle my hand, as if in need of affection.

My Health Visitor came to see me one day, and commented on the stink in my apartment. She didn't come in, and suggested that I employ a council operative to kill the thing. Perhaps she thought I had rats in the place. I shuddered at the thought of having it killed, although I could see from her point of view that that was exactly what I should do. I had grown used to the smell, though the cost of washing the things it came into contact with was quite considerable.

Then a strange thing began to happen. I live alone, and while the thing was with me, I was not alone any longer. So I began to put up with the inconvenience in exchange for its company. It was another creature in the house; a companion, if you like. I got used to its little ways, and in some ways it was rather sweet; the way it would come to me, all trusting and affectionate. I decided it could stay.

Things changed on the day it bit me. It wasn't just a playful nip, as a puppy might do – this was done with bared fangs; a really savage bite that pierced my hand to the bone, leaving me faint-headed with pain and shock. Strangely, it didn't bleed much, but the pain was agonising. Although I had lashed out at the thing, as one does when attacked, it stood its ground, then rolled over onto its back in a gesture of submission. I didn't touch it.

Why had it bitten me? It must have been my fault; something I had done unwittingly. What, I never knew. Maybe it was ill, or I hadn't guessed its needs correctly. I took more care after that not to upset it. It was all friends then, smoothly inching its way forward on to my lap, wanting to be petted and fussed. The wound on my hand throbbed and ached, and finally festered so much that I had to bind it up in a tight bandage and bathe it daily with TCP.

I thought it was my pet; that it would be grateful for the shelter and food and kindness I gave it, but not at all. The more solicitous I became, the more it seemed to despise me. Yet, when I least expected it, the thing would creep out from whichever corner it was hiding in, and insist I stroke it while it licked my hand. I was always very fearful when it did that, and kept the bitten hand well away from it.

Yet strangely, it did seem to need me. The small red eyes would look quite sorrowful if I was doing something else, and I would have to give it attention again or risk being bitten. I began to feel that I had a special relationship with it; as if no one else could possibly understand it.

How wrong I was! I discovered last week that it had also been going next door, and the woman there had been giving it chicken livers. Chicken livers! It came back carrying a small, bloody bundle of the stuff, and gave me a filthy look as it passed me on the step, as if to say that it didn't approve of the way I was treating it, and next door was far better.

Well, I ordered dozens of chicken livers after that, and prawns (which I couldn't really afford), to see if it would make any difference. The thing refused to eat them! I tried everything – being attentive, ignoring it, shooing it with a duster from the corner where it had made a nest in the lounge; even, I'm ashamed to say, trapping it in an old birdcage. I had to let it out again immediately. I didn't like the way it was looking at me, so reproachful and hurt. It didn't seem to care how much it was upsetting me. It continued to nip me whenever it felt like it, then spread its slime and stink all over my bed, until finally something snapped. And still it went next door to eat, avoiding me when I tried to waylay it with enticing morsels, even kicking over the little silver bowls of cream and salmon I had hoped would tempt it, with a contemptuous flick of its back legs. Yes, I bought cream and salmon for it. I know it was foolish, but I really wanted to please it. So it really hurt when it scorned what I was offering and went next door instead. Finally, I was angry.

Right, I thought, *that's enough! It can go and live next door if it likes it there so much.*

I stood by the door and told it to go. But, you know, the creature refused to leave. It wormed around my legs and licked my ankle and became all playful and charming.

Anyway, I've had enough now. It's driven all my visitors away with its smell and bad habits, and the feeding is driving me crazy. It still goes next door and doesn't seem to understand how upsetting I find this. And it bit me again today, badly. I'll have to go to the doctor this time about it. I haven't been out of the house since it arrived. Partly, I'm afraid of what I might find when I get back. Besides, it takes me all my time to clean up after it. But my hand is extremely sore. It's so swollen I can't pick anything up with it, and it throbs all the time. I'll have to let the doctor see it.

It's watching me now from behind the door with its evil little ruby eyes, waiting to see what I lay out for it. It's got something in its mouth this time. What is it? Oh, that is disgusting! There'll be complaints, for sure. People will go to the Town Hall. The police will be called. But it's not my fault; I did the best I could to stop it and I've been a victim too. Look at this finger.

I'll open the door now and wait for it to go next door again. Then I'll shut the door and lock it, jam old rags under it and stop it getting back in here. But it's looking at me with its head to one side, pleading and sorrowful, and it's coming over for a nuzzle. Ah, it doesn't mean any harm. Poor little thing!

It's dropped the thing it had in its mouth, which looks suspiciously like a baby's finger. I'll get the dustpan and clean it up. It's gone to curl up in the living room now, I'll bet, which means I'll have to wash the sofa cover again. Damn nuisance.

No, it has to go. I'll give it until the end of the week, then I'll boot it out. The trouble is, I know what will happen: it'll roll over onto its back and be all pathetic and affectionate, and I'll give in again. It can wind me round its little finger.

AUTHORS' BIOGRAPHIES

JOSEPH DEGAND
SUGAR CUBE

Joseph Degand is a full-time marketer and publicist, with a passion for writing fiction in his spare time. He lives in Lincoln UK with his wife, Heather, but is originally from New Jersey, USA. This is his second published fictional piece; however, he has written several other stories and a novella that he is excited about sharing with the world in the future. Joseph finds inspiration for his writing in a variety of ways; mostly by considering the "What Ifs" of everyday life.

SARAH DIXON
BEYOND FICTION

Sarah Dixon is a prolific writer of short stories, usually Science Fiction or Fantasy but always with a hint of wonder. After spending her life wanting to write, but never reaching her own lofty standards, she read the advice "Finish first, edit later" and finally made it to the end of a chapter. She hasn't stopped since.

A wife and mother of two, it was the desire to write stories that challenged the lure of video games and led her to write her first children's novel: Alfie Slider vs the Shape Shifter is an action adventure for 9 to 12-year-olds, out in late 2016 from SilverWood books.

When not writing, Sarah enjoys working with schools to engage children through creative writing, including delivering a workshop about social commentary in Science Fiction, titled "How Aliens Changed the World".

You can find out more about Sarah at her website:

www.sarahdixonwriter.com

PAULINE E. DUNGATE
SPIRIT OF THE FOREST

Pauline has published a number of stories over the years. She also writes poetry and reviews for sites such as SFCrowsnest and the BFS, under the name Pauline Morgan, and has been a judge for the Arthur C. Clarke and Rubery Awards. She lives in Birmingham (UK) with a husband and a vast collection of books. Other than reading and writing, clement weather often sees her tending the garden. Since retirement from teaching, she has been able to travel to exotic places such as Nepal, Armenia and Papua New Guinea, mostly in search of butterflies to photograph. The places in Ecuador featured in her story are real and were visited a couple of years ago. An earlier story about Hunter and Phoebe appeared in Pulp Heroes 2, published by Alchemy Press. Currently, she and Peter Coleborn of Alchemy Press are editing a volume of stories which is a tribute to friend, and fellow writer, Joel Lane.

KIM GRAVELL
MISTRESS OF FORTUNE

Kim Gravell lives a dangerous life; which is to say she has an artery-clogging, deskbound job as a marketing manager for a global technology company, compounded by a writing habit which leads to her spending even more hours chained to her PC. To counteract this, she practices Shotokan karate, yoga and also runs (slowly).

Her own writing style has been described variously as dark, gripping, descriptive and eloquent. Most of her work contains a strong paranormal or fantasy element, often woven into contemporary settings. She is the author of two paranormal fantasy novels: The Demon's Call and Child of the Covenant, set in present day mid-Wales, as well as several prize-winning short stories.

For further information on Kim's writing, or to purchase her books, visit kimgravell.com.

SARAH HITCHCOCK
PURE

Sarah Hitchcock lives and works in a small town in the west of England. Although she calls the west home, she grew up in the south in a large town squashed between the Downs and the sea. She lives alone, unless you count a small freshwater shrimp that appears to be immortal.

Science Fiction, Fantasy, the unfamiliar, and subverting fairy tales, are how she likes to examine and explore the human condition: a way of turning the real world over a bit and giving it a poke to see if something new crawls out.

She has self-published a novel for older children, called Stan and the Enchantress, and is working on her first novel for adult readers, set in a dystopian future.

DAVID STEVEN MALONE
THE NAUTILUS SHELL

David Steven Malone is a baker and chef de partie from Strathblane, Stirlingshire. He studied Theology and Philosophy at The University of Glasgow, while developing his passion for creative writing. 'The Nautilus Shell' is his first published work, which he is now developing into a novella. If you wish to follow his current writing, you can visit www.blackportmanteau.wordpress.com. This features the blog for the "found diary" of Ronald Vickery, Professor of Folklore and Mythology, All Hallows College, Oxbridge, as compiled by the professor's granddaughter, Matlida Groves. In turn, this acts as the central campaign for his forthcoming novel, 'The Orchard Girl', due for release in September 2017. David also writes under the pseudonym for the blog, Matilda Groves, on Facebook, managing the page, "Black Portmanteau", and on Twitter, under the handle @portmanteaulore.

NINA ORAM
THE SESSION
(WINNING STORY)

Originally from the south of England, Nina Oram lives in the west of Ireland with her Irish partner and their newly acquired stray: a black, witchy cat called Cara. Nina gave up her dream of being a writer long ago, but the beauty and bleakness of her home, along with its connectedness to an ancient history, reawakened her childhood love of myths and legends, megalithic tombs and standing stones. The darkness fascinates her, wherever she finds it.

While continuing to write short stories, Nina is currently working on her first horror book. As with all her work, it plays with the idea that ancient myths and legends are still with us, lying largely undetected beneath the science and veneer of the modern world. More details of Nina's work can be found at Nina Oram, on Wordpress.

JOANNA RICHARDSON
THE WELL-DECEIVED

Of Anglo-Norwegian heritage, and a lifelong devotee of science-fiction, Jo Richardson studied the next best thing at university, ultimately completing a doctorate in molecular biology. A professional research scientist for over ten years, she now teaches biology in higher education. She is particularly interested in the intersection of science and science-fiction, and how the two inform and inspire each other. She blogs on this and other matters at www.liminalt.wordpress.com.

JANE STEWART
THE RAVEN
(WINNING ILLUSTRATION)

Jane has loved drawing and painting, ever since she was young. After training in graphic design and illustration at Suffolk College for three years she worked in publishing and reprographics, mainly producing camera-ready artwork.

Nowadays her favourite media are pencil and acrylics. Her work is about seeing the ephemeral in the landscape. She understands this in terms of myth and Pagan tradition, which helps provide a framework and a starting point for ideas. Today, being in nature and around horses, continues to ground, nurture and inspire her.

She continues to take private commissions and has exhibited work in Reading, Glastonbury, Belfast, Manchester, London and Spain. She lives and works in Reading, with her partner, a cat and an ex-polo pony called Lenny. You can find her work at the Abbey Muse Art Gallery (formerly the Hidden Gem) in Glastonbury and at art shows, bike shows and craft fairs in Berkshire.

You can find out more on www.facebook.com/ArtEpona and http://www.artepona.deviantart.com/

BARBARA STEVENSON
THE ONE-ARMED BANDIT

Barbara Stevenson is a veterinary surgeon and writer, living with various animal companions in Orkney. She writes mainly short stories and sketches, with the odd silly poem thrown in. Some of her short stories have been published in anthologies and, in 2014, she had a couple of sketches performed in the Tron theatre in Glasgow. Her first novel will be out in February 2016, with Yolk Publishing. She is currently working on a murder series set in Neolithic Orkney. As well as writing, she enjoys walking, music and reading - preferably works which are a little off-centre.

You can follow Barbara on Twitter: @Boo2111 or on Facebook as Babs Stevenson.

Valentine Williams
Pet

Valentine Williams (Mary) lurks in a Shropshire cottage with a well under the floor and writes dark fiction.

She was commissioned to write two self-help books resulting from her work in mental health and has since published four novels, some poetry and a collection of short stories: Unconfirmed Reports From Out There.

Her latest novel, Losing It, has been published by Tirgearr Press. She has a background in teaching and psychotherapy. She has four sons but no cat.